The Apache dove for Clint and his knife sliced for Clint's underbelly. The blade scraped hard against his belt buckle and slashed down through the holster and his sixgun.

Clint backed up knowing he should have been disemboweled. "Come and get it," he said, trying to rouse his own flagging spirits. "Or better yet, why don't we shake hands and pretend we are friends? You go your way, I'll go mine. Peace, huh?"

The Indian snarled and slashed again. He did not seem at all interested in palavering about friendship.

Clint slashed at him with the broken limb and the Apache ducked. During the split-second that Clint was off balance, the Apache lunged in for the kill. Clint saw it, knew he was completely exposed, and that a death blow was coming his way. He did the only thing he could do to save his life—as he fell, the Gunsmith drew his gun and put a bullet through the Apache's brain.

Clint listened to the retort of his sixgun echo through the silent mountains . . .

Don't miss any of the lusty, hard-riding action
in the Jove Western series, THE GUNSMITH

And coming next month:

THE GUNSMITH #74: PLAINS MURDER

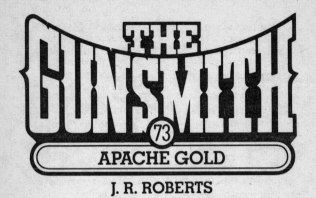

# THE GUNSMITH

## 73

### APACHE GOLD

## J. R. ROBERTS

JOVE BOOKS, NEW YORK

THE GUNSMITH #73: APACHE GOLD

A Jove Book/published by arrangement with
the author

PRINTING HISTORY
Jove edition/January 1988

ISBN: 0-515-09380-7

Jove Books are published by The Berkley Publishing Group,
200 Madison Avenue, New York, New York 10016
The name "JOVE" and the "J" logo
are trademarks belonging to Jove Publications, Inc.

PRINTED IN THE UNITED STATES OF AMERICA

10  9  8  7  6  5  4  3  2  1

# ONE

The Gunsmith figured he had found paradise in the Sangre de Cristo Mountains of northern New Mexico. He had a beautiful dancehall singer named Lotta Cooper as a girlfriend and more gunsmithing business than he needed to pay his bills. When a man had all the honest work he needed or wanted in the daytime, and about as much good loving as he needed or wanted at nighttime, then he had no right to complain about the small, everyday little aggravations that afflict all living individuals.

The town of Union City, New Mexico, suited him right down to the ground. For one thing, even though it was July, the mountain weather was cool, and he liked the scent of the Sugar Cone and Jeffrey Pines. And every few days, he would take an afternoon off, grab his fishing rod and some bait, and head for a racing mountain stream to catch a creel full of fighting speckled or rainbow trout.

Once in a while, he'd even get Lotta to come along, though, mostly, she liked to sleep during the daytime and

sing and dance for the hard-living gold and silver miners at
night. Everyone said that Lotta was the most beautiful saloon girl in New Mexico; Clint figured Lotta was also one
of the wealthiest. The only problem with Lotta was that she
attracted men like bees to a flower. To make matters worse,
the closer a man got to Lotta, the better she looked and
smelled, and the more they wanted her. Lotta was filled out
in all the right places. She had blond hair and the bluest
eyes under the longest lashes Clint had ever seen on any
woman. To watch her sway the length of Union City was to
see normally observant men drive their freightwagons over
the boardwalk and cowboys and miners stumble blindly
into hitching rails, posts, and each other.

Besides being overly trusting and a little loose in the
brain-box, Lotta had one major fault: She was incurably
flirtatious. Oh, she was loyal enough—to a point—but
she liked the attention of the opposite sex and saw nothing
wrong with batting her pretty eyelashes or wiggling her
nice little caboose at men. And sometimes, that could
create some real problems. Especially when the men were
brash or foolish or even too ignorant to recognize Clint
Adams as the Gunsmith, a man who had never been out-
drawn or outgunned in an even, one-on-one stand-up gunbattle.

Clint was not a jealous man. He had never shown any
indication that he wanted to marry Lotta or any other
woman. He liked his freedom without strings, but when he
was out with a woman he never flirted, and he expected
Lotta to play by those same honorable rules. Usually, she
slipped. And sometimes, the Gunsmith had to come down
hard on some oversexed miner or cowboy. Such individuals had to understand that an intelligent man needed to
measure the size of his brain against the size of his penis
and decide which spoke louder and made better sense.

Like now, for example. Clint and Lotta were sitting in

the Bulldog Saloon, enjoying Lotta's fifteen-minute break from her dance routine, and three miners were drooling and ogling her as if she were a damned roast turkey and they were starving for meat. Now that was fine—even expected—when Lotta was up on stage jumping around and singing. But when she was enjoying a quiet moment with the Gunsmith, there was just no damned excuse for rudeness, and the Gunsmith was getting more irritated by the minute.

Lotta leaned forward across their table and sweetly kissed Clint on the nose. "Now, honey," she said, almost spilling her big, beautiful breasts out on the table for everyone in the room to see, "don't you pay any attention to those three nice boys. They're just having a little fun."

"I know," Clint said, "and the air is free to breathe and to look across, but they're starting to rub me the wrong way."

"They're a little drunk or they'd know better than to ogle your girl."

Lotta reached under the table and stroked Clint's thigh. His anger evaporated.

"Besides," Lotta cooed, "they're coarse and dirty fellows, only the youngest one with the blond hair and dimple in his cheeks is the least bit cute. Well, the big one has wonderful shoulders and I love that cleft in his jaw, but. . . ."

Clint shook his head and stopped listening. Maybe it was time to find another woman. Trouble was, with Lotta in town, he would always be reminded of their nights together and how, no matter how frustrated he'd get at her sometimes, she generally made it worth the aggravation. And she really did not flirt to irritate him. It was just the way she was. Like reading palms. Somewhere in her murky past, Lotta Beaver had been under the influence of a gypsy woman. The woman had fouled her impressionable mind with much nonsense, some of it crazy, some not. To this day, Lotta still believed in reading tea leaves and palms. Hell, she thought nothing of grabbing some big miner's callused paw and flopping it knuckles down on a table and then tell the man his future—for ten dollars. She probably averaged fifty dollars a day, and Clint doubted that even one of her clients heard a single word of her rosy predictions. Instead, they would be totally mesmerized by Lotta's bulging, lily-white cleavage straining at her low-cut dress. Lotta knew full well they weren't as interested in their own future as they were in peeking down the front of her dress; it amused her so much that, right in the middle of her palm reading, she would throw in something like, "And this line says you will fall a hundred feet down an abandoned mine shaft in two hours and your body will never be found."

And the miner would just lick his lips, and pant, "Uh-huh, uh-huh, don't stop now, Miss Cooper. Please don't stop!"

To Clint's way of reckoning, it was kind of amusing but also kind of pathetic. It was also very profitable.

"Jeezus!" the first ogling miner said. "I would give a year's wages for one night with that Cooper woman. I would walk barefoot through a den of vipers and eat glass, too!"

The youngest one sipped his whiskey, then said loudly, "After I had made love to Lotta Cooper, I would slice off my horse-sized balls, have them pickled in brine and give them to her as a souvenir. 'Cause after having her, any other woman would be so much a disappointment I might as well be gelded."

The two looked to their partner, the giant with the huge rack of shoulders and blacksmith's arms. "What would you give up, Abe?"

The man belched drunkenly and raised his glass up before his eyes. He looked at the amber liquid and then over at Lotta. "I would even give up whiskey," he vowed. He upended his glass, clenched his teeth, and pounded his mighty fist on the bar for a refill.

"Jeezus," the first man said, awed by Abe's statement.

"My God, Abe," the youngest man swore, "that *is* something."

Clint glared across the table at Lotta. She was smiling at the three men, clearly humbled by their high flattery. "I'll just bet that's one of the finest bunch of compliments any three men have ever uttered to womanhood," she said breathlessly. "Clint, excuse me, but I'm going to sing them a love song and dedicate it to their kind hearts."

Clint groaned. "Their hearts haven't a damned thing to do with it! Move it down about two feet."

Lotta wasn't listening to him. "I gotta sing them a song."

"What about tonight?"

"Come get me at two and we'll go for a buggy ride out to Soldier Creek and have us a swim."

Clint brightened. There was a full moon out tonight and swimming with Lotta Cooper on a summer night and then making love to her on a warm sandbar was about as good as things got in this world.

"All right," he said, "go sing them a song. But I'm going to finish my drink and make sure they don't try to tear your dress off and rape you right on the stage. Any man who'd give up whiskey or his 'horse-sized balls' has got to be seriously addled."

"Clint!"

The Gunsmith smiled impishly. "Only funning you, Lotta. But I just hope that you'd never ask me to do that."

"Of course I wouldn't," she said, kissing him again so that the three rough miners would know that she belonged to him and that they had better behave themselves. She liked to flirt, but she did not like to be mauled, and she could screech and claw like a Rocky Mountain catamount when drastic action was required.

"All right, boys!" Lotta called as she hopped up on the stage, "I am going to sing a love song called, "Love Is an Itch You Can't Scratch," and I know you'll all like it."

The crowd in the saloon quieted. Lotta only sang about five songs a night because she said she was preserving her voice for the opera, though her voice was scratchy as a fiddle, and she could not sing worth spit. But when you had blond hair, big blue eyes, and big . . . well, who cared if she couldn't sing.

The piano player hit a lick and stumbled over the keys. When he played, everything sounded about the same. Clint winced to hear the words of the song, one of her worst efforts about a man who never stopped scratching because he had never gotten over a childhood love. It was a drippy song and the man that wrote it must have composed it as a joke. How it ever got on paper and set to music was a mystery.

"Love is a. . . ."

Clint drank and watched the men watching Lotta. She had the power to spellbind the poor devils, and that was for certain. Mouths hanging open, tongues hanging out.

"Abe!"

Clint twisted around just in time to see the stupid-looking giant miner take a running leap at the stage. He caught his toe on the lip of it and crashed at Lotta's feet. Then he reached out and grabbed her and jerked her to the floor.

"Clint!" she cried as she hit the floor and bounced.

Abe was not big on finessing women. He simply reached under Lotta's dress, grabbed her pantaloons and yanked them down to her ankles as he fumbled at the buttons on his trousers.

"Clint!"

Clint was coming. He was out of his chair and springing across the saloon. "Get off of her!" he bellowed.

But Abe was a man possessed with lust. He had finally gotten his trousers unbuttoned and when Clint reached him, he was ready to rut. Clint drew his gun and, at the very last moment, decided not to shoot the man through the buttocks as he deserved. So instead, Clint slashed the barrel of his sixgun down across the back of Abe's big, shaggy head.

The man grunted and collapsed on Lotta, who was scratching his face up pretty bad. "Get him off me!" she cried. "He's crushing me to death!"

Clint holstered his sixgun and grabbed Abe by the arm with both hands. It was like dragging an ox off poor Lotta.

"Clint, look out!"

Clint spun around and saw a bottle of whiskey come flying at his face. He saw Abe's two friends leaping at him, but then the bottle struck him between the eyes and he did not see anything anymore. The last thing he heard was gunshots and Lotta screaming his name.

Jesus Christ, Clint thought as he felt himself go spinning off toward a dark abyss, I've been shot dead.

# TWO

Clint dimly heard the doctor complain, "I still think he'd be better off just going to his room and getting a good night's sleep."

"Nonsense!" Lotta argued. "What he really needs is a good cool swim to revive him and prevent a headache." Her buggy whip cracked, and Clint's aching head slammed against the side of the buckboard as Lotta set the team in motion.

"Ouch!" he groaned.

"I'm sorry, dear," Lotta said, peering back over her shoulder at the Gunsmith. "That stuffy old doctor gave me headache powders for you, but I know that a good swim and a little lovemaking is what will set you right again."

"Lotta, my head! Why are you driving so fast?" Clint groaned.

"The truth?"

"Sure!"

"The saloon owner was the one that saved you from a

beating tonight. You know that Sheriff Houser wouldn't have kept them miners from tearing you limb from limb."

That part of it was true enough. Sheriff Bert Houser of Union City was an incompetent coward who was too frightened to venture out of his office at night and make the rounds. Bert was pushing sixty and the way that he acted, he wanted to live until he topped a hundred. The man was reported to have once been a real good lawman, but that was twenty years and a couple of bullet wounds ago. Now, Bert was just hanging onto a steady paycheck.

Clint sat up as the buckboard charged down the dirt road on the way to Soldier Creek. The wagonbed was tossing him all over the place and making his head pound like an Apache's drum. "I still don't understand why you are driving so damned fast!"

"Because I heard Abe say that he and his two friends were going to find you alone and cut off your . . ." Lotta pushed on, "Well, something we *both* enjoy and treasure, my dear."

"Abe said that? The giant?"

"Yeah. The one whose skull you should have cracked open with that gunbarrel of yours."

"Damn," Clint muttered. "I'd hoped he would sober up and realize that he got out of hand. He owes *me* the apology."

"Well, that's not how he figures it," Lotta said as they swept down the rutted road. "And I just figured they would be paying your hotel room a visit."

"If they take anything of mine, they're dead men!"

"Oh, Clint, you know that you don't kill anyone for small things. Now just settle down. I brought us a little picnic basket of beer and pickles, a little of Arnie Mendoza's sourdough bread, and some of those red-hot chilis you like. We can spend the night, and when we ride back in the morning, everyone will be sober and back to work, and things will be fine again."

"You shouldn't have sang them that stupid song," Clint groused, sitting up but feeling as if his head were splitting. "Slow down!"

Lotta pulled the horses down to a fast trot, enough so that the buckboard no longer felt as if it were about to fly apart. Clint climbed over the back of the seat and took the lines from her and then pulled the sweaty team of horses down to a walk.

"Clint," Lotta said, "they could be hunting for us."

Clint was not worried in the least. "They wouldn't come riding out in the night all the way to Soldier Creek. They probably don't even own horses. They were miners, Lotta. Miners walk on their own feet, cowboys and the rest of the civilized people ride horses or wagons."

"But there's a full moon out tonight," she argued. "It would almost be like hunting for you in the daylight."

Clint smiled. "Relax. As long as I've got my. . . . Where's my gun!"

Lotta clamped her hand over her mouth. "Oh my gosh! I took it off at the doctor's office, and it must still be hanging on his coatrack."

Clint shook his head and gnashed his teeth in silent fury. This girl would be the death of him yet. "And I don't suppose you are carrying a sixgun."

"Only my derringer."

"One bullet is not much help against three men," Clint grumbled.

"I do carry a couple of extra bullets."

Clint relaxed a little. "Never mind. We won't need them. Like I said, those three miners don't have horses, and they won't leave their whiskey until they pass out— which has likely happened by now anyway."

Lotta snuggled up closer to him. "It was wonderful the

way you came charging in so big and strong to save me tonight. I can't remember when a man ever did that for me so— so gallantly, Clint sweetie."

"I did it for you about three weeks ago at the Green Lizard Saloon when you flirted with four other drunk miners. Remember?"

"Oh, yeah. Well, this time was even better."

Clint might have expressed a very different opinion, but Lotta Cooper had slipped her cool, soft hand inside his shirt and was fooling around with his chest and other places. So Clint just kept quiet and tried to focus on the pleasure and ignore the headache and his growing exasperation with Lotta. The woman meant well and she was a dazzler, but she was dangerous to be around. Clint figured he had had about all the free-for-alls he wanted or needed. Being Lotta's boyfriend was a highly risky proposition.

"It's so beautiful out tonight, Clint. Aren't you glad I wouldn't listen to the doctor and insisted that he load you in the buckboard for a nice ride and a cool, refreshing swim?"

Clint looked up at the stars. They were always spectacular, high above the Sangre de Cristo Mountains. He felt Lotta Cooper's hands slipping below his belt. She was pretty spectacular, too. "Yeah," he sighed, deciding that things weren't really so bad. "I'm glad that you brought me out here. If I was in bed, I'd probably be asleep, and that's no fun."

Lotta giggled and tweaked him a little. "I just *knew* that getting beaned by a whiskey bottle couldn't slow you down, Gunsmith!"

Clint smiled and guided the buckboard toward a small meadow beside the river. It was their secret place to go fishing, swimming, and fooling around. There was a great big pool of water created by an old abandoned beaver dam. You could have a fine time here and actually see huge trout gliding around in circles down near the base of the watery roots of trees.

Lotta was off her seat and running across the grass like a forest nymph before Clint even touched the ground. He unhitched the team, watered them, and then hobbled both horses and let them feed on the lush meadow grass. Clint liked to think that, if he was going to enjoy the evening, the horses ought to enjoy it, too.

"Hurry up!" she called, stripping down to nothing but her lovely self and sort of dancing around on the riverbank.

Clint just stopped for a minute to admire her. With the glow of moonlight on her lovely white skin, she was about as beautiful as anything a man could wish to see. There was a good deal of the child in Lotta, a sort of innocence that was only half feigned. Lotta Cooper seemed to have the unique ability to glide unscathed through a hard frontier world of saloons, whorehouses, and disapproving wives.

Clint walked over beside her and started to reach for her, but she laughed and jumped out of his grasp. Then, before he could tackle her to the grass, she made a beautiful dive off the bank and hit the water as gracefully as a trout leaping to gobble a mosquito.

Clint shucked off his boots, his empty holster, and then his shirt and pants. He took two big strides and launched himself off the riverbank and struck Soldier Creek with a tremendous splash. He went under the surface of the beaver pond, and when his feet sank into the thick, gooey mud on the bottom, he pushed up and went after Lotta.

"You'll never catch me!" she laughed, swimming only half as fast as her capabilities allowed.

Clint overhauled her at the sand bar and when he grabbed her ankles, he pulled her to him. She pretended to fight. She splashed and made a big fuss, but she was fooling nobody, least of all the Gunsmith.

The cool water was unquestionably refreshing, but Lotta

naked in his arms was intensely stimulating. One minute
they were thrashing in about a foot of water as Lotta pretended a desire to escape, the next minute, the woman was
all over the Gunsmith, showering him with hungry kisses
and arousing him with her lips and tongue.

They rolled up on the sandbar and Lotta, long hair
hanging around her face, climbed on the Gunsmith and
grabbed his stiff flagpole with both hands. Big breasts glistening wetly, she slid down his body and then her warm
mouth took his entire length.

Clint flopped back on the sandbar and dug his fingers
into her hair and rotated her head the way she liked. He felt
her lips glide up and down his pulsating rod, and when he
knew that he could stand it no longer, he rolled her over
and drove himself into her.

She shuddered. She sighed with pleasure and then
wrapped her long legs around his waist as their hips moved
in perfect unison. A fish jumped out of the water to splash
nearby. The leaves of the trees seemed to whisper with
excitement, and Clint rode the slippery beauty under him
with mounting urgency. His mouth covered hers, their
tongues clashed, and their bodies made quickening sounds
as the water around them moved faster.

"Oh . . . oh, Clint . . . please stop!" she moaned.

He did not stop. She always said that, and once he actually had found the willpower to stop and then she had
clawed his buttocks with her fingernails, leaving angry red
marks. She did not want him to stop, she would not let him
stop.

"Clint . . . please . . . please stop!"

That was her way of telling him to move into her even
harder and faster. He rode her like he would have a high-
spirited filly, and she loved it. And when her beautiful legs
lost their strength and fell away to splash helplessly at the

surface of the stream, Clint covered her turgid nipples with his mouth and that drove her absolutely wild.

She lost control. He felt her flat belly begin to quiver and then she was bucking furiously and screaming with joy. Clint let her have his torrent of hot seed; he pumped it deep into her and she begged him not to stop until they finally lay gasping like two beached fish.

When Lotta could catch her breath, she hugged him and kissed him tenderly. "Clint, darling," she whispered in his ear, "you are the best man I ever screwed in my life. The very best."

"Why, thank you," he said as though she had never told him that before, "and you are the most beautiful woman I ever had in Soldier Creek."

She laughed and pushed him off into the current. Clint flopped over and over and when he stood up to wrestle her lovely frame back down on the sandbar, he heard a shout and then the unmistakable blast of a Colt .45.

"It's . . . it's them!" Lotta screamed.

Clint threw himself at her and as more bullets began to stitch the night, they hurled across the sandbar and plunged into the deepest part of the beaver pond.

They went under and when they came back up again, bullets began to pelt the water all around their heads. Clint looked up to see the three miners standing side by side on the riverbank. Drunk, but shooting to kill.

The Gunsmith's first thought was to save Lotta Cooper, but his second thought was to find a way to kill the three of those crazy bastards, once and for all.

# THREE

They swam for the beaver lodge, and when they reached it they ducked behind its mud and logs for protection.

Lotta was out of breath and frightened. "What are we going to do now?"

Clint heard more shouting and the gunfire stopped. He peeked around the lodge and shook his head. "They're riding across the river," he said. "They can come at us from either side, and we'll have no place to hide."

"They can shoot us like fish in a barrel!"

"They don't want to hurt you, Lotta. At least, not until they've had their pleasure. Even drunk, they have to realize I'm going to kill them if I can. They won't stop coming until I'm dead."

"Well, I won't leave you, Clint! So if that's what you're working up to, forget it!"

It had been what the Gunsmith had been about to suggest, but now, he saw the folly of the plan. The three miners would simply begin to rape Lotta knowing he would attempt to come to her aid. And he would have been shot.

"What are we going to do?"

Clint took a deep breath. The dam was a good fifty yards away, and they would probably be shot whenever they had to surface for air. And even if they did reach the dam there was no way that they could climb over it in a big hurry. No, Clint decided, I do not like the odds on that plan, either.

But when he heard a horse and rider splash into the river and begin to swim across, Clint knew that he was running out of time in a big hurry. Once the rider reached the opposite shore and rode down even with the beaver lodge, there would be no place to hide except—inside the lodge itself.

"Don't move," he said, diving under the big structure. The lodge went down deeper than he had expected. And when he did manage to get underneath the thing, the water was so dark and murky that he couldn't see his hand before his face. So he began to jam his fists upward into the base of the lodge, desperately hoping to probe the beavers' entrance.

He ran out of time and surfaced, took three deep breaths, and dove again. This time, he went straight underneath and was successful. He found the opening and shot upward through a slick tunnel. His head popped to the surface, and the first thing he learned was that the inside of a beaver's lodge stunk, and the second thing he learned was that a family of beavers is not happy to welcome intruders into their home.

It was pitch black inside, but the beavers were screeching, chattering, and snapping their teeth so loud that he knew there was a bunch of them, each thoroughly pissed off by his arrival. Clint had nothing but a sharp stick to defend himself with, and a big male beaver could weigh over forty pounds. Clint had no desire whatsoever for one of these big rodents to sharpen its teeth on his skull.

"Easy, boys and girls," he whispered reassuringly. "I am a friend about to bring another friend. But if some of you choose to go for a swim before I return, I won't object to that, either."

Clint took a deep breath and ducked back down the tunnel. He kicked hard and when he shot to the surface, he discovered that he had lost his sense of direction. The two miners who had not crossed Soldier Creek had him dead-to-rights but were so startled that Clint was able to duck and swim around to rejoin Lotta before they could unleash a volley of bullets.

"My God!" she cried. "You were down there so long that I thought you had drowned."

She was crying, shivering, and nearly in a panic. Clint could see why. The rider was across the creek and breaking through the trees to come opposite his friends. Once in position, he and Lotta would be caught helpless in a crossfire. "Take a deep breath and hold my hand, Lotta. We're going to visit some furry friends."

"Jeezus! You mean they're all inside this thing?"

"They are. Inside is where all smart beavers go in an emergency. Right now, we are going to do exactly the same. So just stick with me. We go down about. . . ."

Clint would have liked to explain but the horseman burst out of the trees and unleashed a bullet that was much too close for comfort. It thudded into the lodge and sent mud and bark flying across the water.

"Let's dive!" Clint shouted.

They dove, hearing the small plinking sounds of bullets cutting through the surface of the beaver pond. Down they went, and Clint kept his hand clamped on Lotta's arm, which made swimming tough indeed. But it was essential that she be led to the upward tube into the lodge. Otherwise, she would either get trapped under the lodge and drown, or risk being shot when she clawed in terror back to the surface.

Lotta began to panic almost as soon as they were under the lodge. Clint could feel her begin to tug at his arm, and the tugs became frantic jerks as her air supply ran lower.

Just a little farther, he thought. Come on, Lotta, just a little farther! He had feared this might happen. Being under the lodge in black water without a sure knowledge of where the beaver opening was to be found would be terrifying for anyone. If Clint lost the opening, they might both get tangled up in the sharp sticks and mud, and drown.

But Clint knew exactly where he was going, and he knew that he could not allow Lotta to break free and return to the surface. So he held onto her even when she began to fight wildly. When his fist punched up into the beavers' entry tube, Clint sank his feet into the mud on the floor of the pond and shoved Lotta up that hole to greet the beaver family.

He counted off three seconds and with is own lungs burning and ready to explode with fire, he drove himself up to join her.

Lotta grabbed his head the moment it slid up between her big, chilled breasts. "Listen to them!" she cried. "They're snapping their teeth and getting ready to eat us alive!"

Clint pushed his shoulders up through the tube and held his woman tightly. She was shivering with cold and fear. He did not blame her. The sounds the beavers were making were very threatening.

"Maybe if we just calm down, they'll do the same," Clint said.

"It stinks in here! I think we ought to get the hell outta their house!"

"And greet our three friends with nothing but a handful

of mud to throw? Uh-uh," Clint said. "They'll either figure
we drowned or gave them the slip in the dark water. Either
way, they'll soon tire of this and run out of whiskey. When
they do, then we leave and head back to town."

"What if we have to walk?"

"We can do that if we have to, Lotta."

"Sharp rocks hurt the soles of my feet," she told him.
"You walk and then come back for me with a buggy."

"All right. But right now, we wait."

So they waited, locked tightly together, trying to fric-
tion up a little warmth in absolute darkness in a beaver
lodge with a bunch of ill-tempered, chattering rodents.
What seemed like hours later, Clint squeezed out of the
mud tube and floated lightly to the surface of the pond.

The three miners were gone, but so was their buckboard, their picnic basket, and all their clothes. Clint gritted his teeth. Back in town when he had attacked the trio
for jumping Lotta, well, that was one thing. But now,
coming out to kill a defenseless man taking a night swim,
that was something else entirely.

I'll either kill them, or have the sheriff arrest them for
attempted murder, Clint thought. Either way, they are
going to pay for this night. Pay for it dearly.

Lotta popped to the surface and gasped for fresh air. "I
couldn't stand it inside that place without you for another
single minute!" she cried, throwing her arms around his
neck and holding him. "Are they gone yet?"

Clint nodded. "But so is everything else. Even our
clothes."

Lotta twisted around to peer at the moonlit meadow.
"Those dirty bastards," she swore. "If you don't kill them,
I swear I will!"

"Come on," Clint said, "let's get to shore and dry off in
the grass. I got a long walk ahead of me that I'm sure not
looking forward to."

Lotta suddenly began to giggle. "Yeah," she said, "I hadn't thought of it, but it would mess up a great reputation if the famous Gunsmith came walking into Union City about daybreak naked as a baby and limping from rock bruises."

"Maybe I should send *you*," Clint said, not a bit amused by the image she had conjured up for him.

"Bad idea."

"Why?"

"Because," Lotta told him, "naked, I wouldn't stand a snowball's chance in hell of making it upright."

Clint helped her out of the water. She was shivering but that took nothing away from that magnificent body of hers. "That's true," he conceded, "the first man that saw you would be in real deep trouble."

# FOUR

It was a long, cold walk into town, but the Gunsmith was steaming by the time he limped down the back alley and hobbled into the lobby where the nightclerk was sleeping. Clint took his room key from the pegboard and tiptoed up the staircase to his room.

He was almost there when a man and a woman came stumbling out into the hallway. Seeing the naked Gunsmith, they both stopped and gaped.

"I bet everything on the turn of a card," Clint said, raising his arms and dropping them uselessly beside his bare flanks.

The woman's figure if not her face was familiar. She worked in the red-light district of town, and Clint had seen her around.

"Mister," she said, in a low, husky voice, "you better find some pants to cover that big, dangling thing before it catches pneumonia and dies. Or better yet, bring it by and ask for Lola, and I'll doctor it up for you."

The man burst out laughing, and Clint made a sweeping motion as they passed. He entered his room and dressed quickly. The sun was coming up when he hobbled over to find Sheriff Houser drinking coffee at the local cafe.

Houser looked and acted more like a preacher than a lawman. He had a pink complexion and round, rosy cheeks. Middle-aged and prematurely bald, he spoke too fast and acted too slow.

"I need to talk to you," Clint said, sliding in across the table. Clint motioned for coffee and while the waitress poured, he studied the sheriff with growing conviction that he was wasting his time.

"About what?" Houser already looked worried.

"Three miners that tried to kill Lotta Cooper and me last night out at Soldier Creek."

Houser studied his coffee for so long that Clint thought a fly must have landed in it. Then the man asked, "What were you doing out at Soldier Creek in the dark?"

"With a woman like Lotta Cooper, what do you think!"

Houser actually jumped. He spilled his coffee on his shirt. He raised his hand and said, "Now don't get riled, Gunsmith. But I needed to know."

When the waitress filled his cup, Clint drank the scalding black coffee fast. "I'm in a hurry," he said, knowing that he already should have been out on the road to get poor Lotta, "so I'll only go through this story once, and you had better listen close."

Houser didn't like to be talked down to. But with the Gunsmith, he knew better than to say anything. He listened carefully, his eyes gradually widening as the Gunsmith talked.

"You and her were hiding in a beaver's lodge!"

"Yeah. And when I get back, you and I are going to go over to the Consolidated Mine and find those three men. You'll arrest them for attempted murder . . . or else."

"Else what?" the sheriff asked.

"Or else I'm going to throw your fat ass down an empty mine shaft and kick dirt over your broken body."

The sheriff choked on a mouthful of coffee. "There could be real trouble at the Consolidated," he finally managed to croak. "It's company policy that no one can come on their property or in any way interfere with men who are working down below."

"They can shove company policy!" Clint said harshly. "We're going!"

He stood up and headed for the doctor's office to retrieve his gun.

Finding Lotta was easy, but when he handed her an old horse blanket to wear back to Union City, she erupted in anger. "Couldn't you have at least brought me a dress?"

"Nope. I don't have a key to your room, and I don't own one."

"Then you should have bought one."

"All the stores were closed. Besides," the Gunsmith said, "those three that were after us last night stole my pants and all of my money."

"You got an answer for everything this morning, don't you," she said in a huff.

Clint wrapped the horse blanket around her and helped her up onto the buckboard. Her teeth were chattering, her nose was red and running, and she was sneezing furiously.

"I'm going to die in a stinking horse blanket!" she wailed, tears springing into those big blue eyes. "Not only that, but the whole damn town of Union City is going to see me like this! My reputation will be a joke."

Clint took pity on her. "Go back there and lay down under the blanket," he said, remembering how he had lain in much the same circumstances the night before. "I'll get you to your room without being seen."

Hope shone through the tears. "Promise?"

Clint nodded.

"I . . . kachoo! I . . . love you, kachooo!"

Clint shook his head. It sounded like poor Lotta was going to be indisposed for a while. That was fine, since Clint figured he'd have his hands full arresting big Abe and his two murderous friends. The sheriff wasn't likely to be much help.

Union City was bustling by the time they returned. True to his word, Clint did get Lotta back to her hotel room without being seen, though he almost cold-cocked her, struggling up the back stairs. As soon as Lotta was settled into bed with a stack of clean handkerchiefs, Clint headed for the sheriff's office.

The door was locked even though it was midmorning and that made Clint furious. "Mister, do you have any idea where this chicken-hearted sheriff is hiding?" he asked an old man whittling a stick.

"Left town in a hurry when he heard the Corbett brothers are coming to Union City to kill old Judge Monroe."

"The Corbett brothers? Who are they?"

The old man looked up at the Gunsmith and closed one eye. "Just the meanest, most dangerous sonsabitches in New Mexico is all."

"Why do they want the judge?"

"He sent 'em away to prison for ten years. They swore to kill him when they got out, and that's just what they're going to do. They swore they'd also kill any town sheriff that tried to stop 'em.

"That's why the sheriff left in such a hurry. The minute the news came in over the telegraph wires, the sheriff commenced to shakin' and quiverin' as though he had ants climbin' all over his porky body. Then, he just took off his badge and dropped it in the dirt."

Clint shook his head in disgust. In all the years he had been a sheriff himself, he had never once heard of such a pathetic lawman. "What a coward!"

"Maybe," the old man said as he whittled the soft white stick in his dark-veined hands, "and maybe not. The sheriff, he said that when you came back you wanted him to arrest Abe Holoran and his two friends for attempted murder."

"In addition to no guts, the sheriff had a very loose mouth."

"But he was smart, Gunsmith. He figured out loud that, between the miners and the Corbett brothers, one or the other bunch would ventilate his gizzard. So he left in good health."

The Gunsmith still figured that the sheriff had showed poorly. As long as things were quiet, Houser had accepted a paycheck, but the minute a little trouble came up, wham, he was off and running.

The old man plucked the sheriff's badge out of his pocket and shined it on his sleeve. "Pretty thing, ain't it."

"I guess."

"You wanta borrow it and stand against the Corbett brothers when they come?"

"Nope. I got my own axe to grind with that Abe fella and his two buddies." He checked his gun. "See you later, old timer."

The old man waved his thin stick with one hand and his knife with the other. "You watch that Abe, he's smarter than he looks."

"Thanks, I'll do that," Clint promised.

The Consolidated Mine was the biggest employer in Union City, with a monthly payroll that was said to approach twenty thousand dollars. Clint was greeted by a pair of guards who wore guns and seemed anything but friendly.

"What do you want?" the bigger of the pair asked.

"Three men who work for you," Clint said. "I'm arresting them for attempted murder. One is named Abe Holoran. The other two will likely be close to him."

"See that wooden post yonder?"

Clint turned around and stared at a post about a hundred feet behind him. "Yeah, so what?"

"So walk back and stand the other side of it, off our property. When the shift is over, you can do whatever you have a mind to do. But not here and not now."

Clint studied the pair. He had not slept last night and he was in a short temper. So he just drew the gun on his hip. It wasn't his smoothest or fastest draw, but it was faster than the blink of an eye.

"See this gun?" he aked.

They nodded enthusiastically.

"Take me to Abe Holoran, or I'll stick it in your ears and blow out the cobwebs."

The pair jumped to obey him. Clint figured it was a damn shame that a man just couldn't reason without resorting to pulling his iron. But you could not deny that one gun was sometimes worth a thousand words.

Clint followed the two guards down the ore track. Big ore carts were coming up one every five minutes, pulled by a cable hooked to a huge steam engine. He had been in mines before and expected the Consolidated Mine to be big, but it was even more impressive than he had imagined. The tunnel they traveled down was ten feet high and fifteen feet across. Almost every seventy feet there was a mine station or a shaft leading off where Clint could hear men working with hammers, chisels, and picks. Down each of those new shafts ran a shiny pair of steel rails to bring even more ore up to the surface, where it was dumped into huge tailing piles.

The miners wore little lanterns on their foreheads, so whenever they passed, their illumination bounced off the pitted walls. As they passed a supply station, Clint spied a barrelful of pick handles. He grabbed one and followed along with the pick in his left hand. Down here, Abe and his friends would have the advantage. Clint figured he would use the pick handle if he could, but his gun if it was necessary.

"Stop," he said.

The two guards stopped and stood at attention. Clint caught up with them. "How much farther?"

"Straight ahead about a hundred feet, then the tunnel goes off to the right for about fifty yards. That's where we'll find them."

"You boys had better not warn them. If they run or fight, bullets will be flying. You might accidentally get hit."

The guards understood perfectly. They led Clint right to the three men he wanted.

Clint took Abe first, and he did it by simply walking up behind the giant and smashing him over the head with the pick handle. Abe had been swinging a hammer, and Clint had not wanted to take any chances of winding up on its receiving end.

The other two were working about ten feet away. When they saw Abe fall they whirled, and Clint sent two bullets scorching across the cavern just over their heads.

It worked and yet it was an awful mistake. The bullets ricocheted four times each off the rock walls and sent everyone to the floor. When the ruckus finally died, Clint climbed up and said, "You two and the big fella I slugged are under arrest for attempted murder."

"You can't arrest us!"

"Keep talking," the Gunsmith said, "and I may decide to just shoot you instead."

That settled it. The two went meek as lambs, and Clint had them pitch big Abe into an ore cart and then push him all the way out of the tunnel.

"You're going to jail," he said, "so pick Abe up and let's move."

"Who the hell do you think you are! The sheriff or something!"

Clint shrugged his shoulders. "Maybe I do," he said. "Maybe I do."

# FIVE

Despite his success in capturing the three miners alive within their underground lair, the Gunsmith had every reason to be grim. But as he prodded them out of the Consolidated Mine and marched toward town, he had a nagging suspicion that his problems were going to be compounded by the fact that there was no longer an official sheriff.

But dammit! Just because that cowardly Houser had run scared with the first breath of an ill wind was no damned reason why these three men should get away with attempted murder. No reason at all! They had tried to kill him and poor Lotta and almost succeeded.

The two miners were having a hard time of carrying the giant, Abe Holoran. Abe probably weighed close to two hundred and fifty pounds, and he was a dead weight. They dropped him twice and banged up the back of his head on the rocky road to Union City.

"Each one of you grab an arm and drag him!" Clint said roughly. "By the time we get to jail the man will be beaten to death the way you two are dropping him every fifty feet."

One of the miners, chest heaving, sweat bursting out across his forehead, managed to wheeze, "Mister Gunsmith, it . . . it was all Abe's idea. We didn't mean to kill you last night. We just wanted to run you off."

"The hell you say," Clint growled. "Tell it to the judge."

"There won't be no judge after the Corbett brothers arrive. He'll be planted in the cemetery."

"Then I'll see that you are tried in his court before they arrive."

The pair exchanged glances. "Abe was a good friend of Harry and Williard Corbett. Them Corbetts will free all of us from jail."

"He and his brother will have to go through me first," Clint said. "And that might not be so easy."

The pair grabbed Abe by the arms and roughly dragged the giant forward along the road. The heels of his boots left twin tracks in the dirt. Word of Clint's action had already preceded them into Union City. Townfolks had gathered to wait and see the Gunsmith and the three tamed hellers. And now, as Clint entered Main Street, the boardwalks were lined with people gawking at the curious sight of two men dragging an unconscious giant through the dirt.

"Whatcha gonna do with 'em now!" was the most common cry thrown in Clint's direction.

"They're under arrest, and they're going to be tried for attempted murder and general unruliness," he answered at first.

"But there ain't even no sheriff to watch 'em!"

"I know that."

"And there ain't even gonna be no judge alive to try them."

"The hell there won't be," Clint said with heat in his voice.

By the time they reached the sheriff's locked and abandoned office, the Gunsmith was worn out telling those people the same answers to the same stupid questions over and over. Being short-tempered at that point, he simply drew his gun and shot the doorlock to pieces. The people drew back, a little shocked at his lack of patience.

"The locksmith could have opened it," Mr. Ronald Beamon, the town's mayor, complained. "That's public property, you know."

Clint ignored the man and used his gun to motion his prisoners inside. Fortunately, the jail cell keys were hanging on a nail or else Clint might have lost this temper and done something regretful.

Half the town squeezed into the sheriff's office to watch Clint lock the three men up tight. He turned around and handed the mayor the jail cell keys.

"They're all yours, Beamon."

But the mayor blew out his round cheeks and said, "Now, wait just a minute, Gunsmith! You're overstepping your bounds this time. You've no right to make an arrest, and this town has no sheriff to hold those men in custody."

"I made a citizen's arrest and this town has a solid jail cell. Getting another sheriff to watch over these three until Judge Monroe can try and sentence them to prison is your problem, Mayor."

Mayor Beamon was a short and aggressive little mining engineer who had arrived from the East. He was mentally quick and not a man to be shunted aside in an argument. "I don't think you understand. Union City is unwilling to fund the care of three prisoners for any length of time. We are raising funds for a city hall. Not for caring for three prisoners."

"You had better change your thinking," Clint warned. "The lawless must be punished and your budgets be damned."

"Spoken like an ex-lawman, Mr. Adams, and not a realist in terms of city budget. And as for hiring a new sheriff to replace Houser, may I demonstrate a reality to you?"

Clint nodded.

Beamon turned around to face the packed roomful of people. He climbed up on the sheriff's desk so that he could even be seen by those outside and in the street.

"My friends," he called, "as Mayor of Union City, you all know we face a crisis. The Corbett brothers, remembered by some and known to be friends of the men that the Gunsmith has just arrested, are coming to our town. What I am asking for are candidates for our new sheriff. The pay is thirty dollars a month. Those of you who are willing to risk their lives to protect this town, this jail, and these prisoners, please step forward and give me your names and qualifications."

Beamon smiled confidently and waited. As he'd expected, not a single man, either in the jail or standing out in the street, stepped forward.

"Hell," one of them said, "working for the Consolidated Mine pays forty dollars and at least you got a fifty-fifty chance of seeing tomorrow's sunrise."

Hearing this, the miners nodded their heads in agreement.

Beamon stepped down from the desk. He smoothed a crumpled piece of paper that he had left his footprint upon and shrugged his narrow shoulders. "Now, Mr. Adams, are you finally aware of the problem?"

"Sure," Clint said, glaring at the crowd with a bad taste growing in his mouth. "The problem is that nobody I see has any guts."

The miners didn't like that comment, but there was enough truth in it and steel in Clint's voice to silence them.

Beamon took a more reasoned line of thinking. "It takes plenty of 'guts' to work a hundred feet underground in a

mine, Mr. Adams. What is lacking here is both the will
and the means to stand up to the Corbett brothers as well as
whoever else might choose to raise hell. Are you looking
for another job?"

"Not a chance," Clint said. "I've paid my dues in a
dozen drafty little offices like this one. I'm retired from
being a lawman and I enjoy gunsmithing."

"Too bad," Beamon said with an audible sigh of resig-
nation. "Then I guess we'll just have to release those prisoners."

He started to step forward, but Clint grabbed him by
the sleeve and said, "You open that cell and let those
three loose, and I'll toss you in there and throw away the
key."

Beamon's aloof little smile evaporated from his porcine
lips. "Now, wait just a minute."

"No, you wait a minute," Clint said, cutting the man
off. "As long as you have a town, you have to have law.
Otherwise, you'll have chaos and murder in the streets.
There are good people who live in Union City. Women,
children, and honest men trying to make a living. But
without a sheriff, this town will degenerate into just another Bodie or some other hellhole. Pretty soon, all the
decent people will pack up their things and run away, leaving only the outlaws to prey upon the miners. And after a
couple of dozen of them are murdered, you'll have lynch-
law."

Clint looked at the crowd rather than just the mayor.
"Any of you men ever been part of a lynch mob?"

A few nodded. A lot more studied their hands and their
feet uneasily, and Clint knew it was because they were
ashamed of what they had done.

"Lynching is a dirty, scarring business. Even when you
have lynched a man guilty as sin, you'll still wake up years
later remembering how he cried and pleaded and then how

he jerked and danced at the end of your rope. It's ugly when its done by a mob. You all know that. But when a man has been properly judged in a court of law and then sentenced to hang, there is no guilt. The law of the land has spoken, and justice has prevailed. There are no dark questions or threads of guilt that ring hollowly through your mind for years and years."

He paused. "And those are the reasons why Union City must have law and order at any price. Mr. Mayor, Union City can't afford *not* to hire a good sheriff."

Two people outside on the boardwalk began to clap their hands loudly. Clint recognized one of them as being Judge Addison Monroe. The other was his pretty young daughter, Miss Judy Monroe, a girl who had never spoken a word to him or even smiled in his direction, until now.

Her smile and that of the dignified old judge suddenly made Clint feel a whole lot better. And when their applause was joined by first a smattering of miners and then the whole danged crowd, Clint was feeling very good indeed. Maybe Union City deserved him for a temporary sheriff after all.

He would give it serious consideration in the days ahead.

# SIX

That evening he visited a very sick and out-of-sorts Lotta Cooper but escaped her short temper as soon as possible. He had a few drinks in the Bulldog Saloon and when he returned to his room, Clint discovered a message had been slipped under his room door. It read:

*Dear Mr. Adams,*
*Please join my father and me for breakfast at our home tomorrow morning at ten o' clock. Your words about law and order were stirring, but your commitment is essential. You must help Union City and my father.*

*Sincerely, Miss Judy Monroe.*

Clint stared at the missive for a long time before he climbed into bed. The last he had heard, the town had hired some old fella to feed the prisoners and watch over them, but no one had stepped forward with an offer to actually become sheriff. Apparently, ten years had not eased the fear of the Corbett brothers from the minds of these people.

But dammit, Clint thought as he laced his fingers behind his head and stared up at his ceiling, I've done more than my share of protecting towns like this one. And if I keep stepping in to carry the responsibility of others, someday I'll slow down on the draw or lose my sense of danger and get killed. Then I'll really be upset.

Clint had seen too many lawmen push their careers past the time when they should have retired to the easy chair. He'd had at least eight or ten old friends who had stayed in the business too long and paid for it with their lives. It was hard to tell a man that his reflexes were starting to slow a little or that, in the heat of a gunbattle, his aim was not quite as quick and as sure as it had been when he was twenty-one.

But counterbalancing the loss of youth was the factor of experience. Youth and raw speed got a lot of young lawmen killed before they were seasoned enough to know when to fight and when to wait until the odds were more favorable.

And finally, there was the judge to think about. So far, everyone seemed to be ignoring the fact that he was the main target for reprisal by the Corbetts. Oh, Clint had heard some empty talk about forming a band of citizen's to protect the old judge. But that was a bunch of bullshit. The men who called the judge their friend and cared enough about him to consider risking their lives were old or else they had never fought in a gunbattle. Those kinds of well-intentioned friends were almost useless. They'd get themselves killed, and they'd do nothing to help the judge.

I can't let the Corbett brothers just come riding in to kill Judge Monroe, Clint thought, knotting his fists at his side. And as long as I'm going to stop them, I had better protect myself and be wearing a badge. That way, any killing will at least be in the line of duty.

When Clint awoke the next morning to shave and take a bath, he felt good because his mind was made up. Miss Monroe had stated plain out that she wanted him to be sheriff and save her father's life. Clint appreciated that approach. Many women might have tried to charm or otherwise manipulate him into saying yes. It showed that Judy Monroe was guileless, and that was a rare quality in the type of women Clint usually met. Lotta, for instance, could charm a snake and had more wiles than an Indian medicine man.

He polished his boots, put on a pressed and starched white shirt and had the hotel Chinaman sponge and press his black frocked coat. By the time he was ready to leave, he had to admit that he looked highly respectable. Not that anyone would ever mistake him for a banker, but he did not look like a man who had earned his living tracking down outlaws and surviving gunfights.

Clint walked past the Orion Hotel where Lotta stayed. Her window was open, and he saw her lace curtains swaying lightly in the morning breeze. He paused, thinking he ought to stop and visit for a moment, but then he heard her begin to sneeze and blow her nose with a loud honking sound.

Clint shook his head with pity and decided to pass without visiting Lotta this morning. He stolled over to Elm Street and walked right up to the judge's fine, two-story stone house with the big iron gate and wrought-iron fence. The rumor was that the judge had come from Tennessee where his family had owned a rich plantation and raised Thoroughbred horses. That part of it might be true, because the judge's stable had four of them.

Clint knocked and the door was opened by a colored maid who smiled and said, "Welcome to the Monroe residence, Mr. Adams. The Judge and Missy are waitin' for you at the table."

She took the Gunsmith's hat and then looked at the gun and holster he wore. "You won't be needing that in here, suh."

Clint unbuckled it and gave it to the smiling woman. "What's your name?"

"Milly," she said, acting pleased that he had shown enough interest to ask.

"Well, I'm glad to meet you, Miss Milly."

"The pleasure is all mine. You a famous man, suh. And we are countin' on you to protect our dear judge."

Clint nodded. He followed the maid inside and was led into a spacious dining room. At one end of a huge oak table with no fewer than twenty antique chairs sat the judge, who rose and came around to shake the Gunsmith's hand. At the other end sat Miss Judy, in a white blouse with her black hair tied up prettily with a pink ribbon.

She looked just as Clint supposed any southern belle might look, and she fit in perfectly with the rich tapestries, the heavy crystal chandeliers, and the huge painting depicting life on a southern plantation. One look around the room and at Judge Addison Monroe and his daughter told Clint the rumors about the man had probably been true. The judge even looked like a southern gentleman. Tall and spare with wavy gray hair, he had a certain elegance that was not often seen in the West among men who cut wood, planted crops, or chased cows as part of their daily livelihood. When they shook hands, the judge's hand was soft, his fingers as long and slender as those of a concert pianist.

The judge said, "I'm afraid I have a confession to make, sir. I was aware—both my darlin' Judy and I were aware —that you were a gunfighter and an outlaw-tamer. We assumed you were a man of courage and conviction, but we did not realize you were also a man who is skilled in the art of elocution."

Clint almost asked what that meant but was saved when the judge answered the question by adding, "Yes, Mr. Adams. You have fine oratorical skills. You should have been a politician."

"No, thank you. I have no heart for making promises I can't deliver on."

"Nor have I," the judge said. "There is too much sacrifice of honor. And honor, that is a man's most prized possession, don't you agree, sir?"

"Next to his wife and children, his best friend and his horse, I suppose it is," Clint said in agreement.

Judy smiled but the judge was not amused. "I think you are humoring me, sir."

"Clint," the Gunsmith said. "If we can't go by first names, I'm not going to enjoy our breakfast together."

"Clint it is, then. You may call me Addison, and my daughter is Miss Judy."

Clint bowed and when the Monroes took their places, he found himself suddenly undecided about which one of the many chairs he was supposed to sit in.

"Please sit beside my father," Judy said. "It would please him."

Clint would rather have pleased the girl, but he did as he was asked. Miss Milly arrived to serve them hot biscuits under chicken gravy, scrambled eggs, pork chops, fresh melon, and strawberry jam. The coffee was rich—better than anything Clint had ever tasted—and they ate largely in silence, making small talk until Milly cleared the table and they all moved into the judge's study.

"I've never seen so many books," the Gunsmith said, admiring the floor to ceiling bookcases filled with interesting old tomes.

The judge was pleased. "They are all that is left of my..." he hesitated, and his voice trailed away.

Clint frowned in bewilderment and looked to the girl. She forced a smile and offered him and her father Cuban cigars, and the awkward moment passed.

It was Judy who finally broached the true reason for this meeting. "What we most sincerely wish to do," she began, "is to hire you to protect this town and my father. But despite all that you might think and these rather... rather nice surroundings, we are really not in a position to pay you well."

Clint blinked and his astonishment must have shown because the girl rushed on. "I have a few pieces of jewelry and...."

"Whoa!" the Gunsmith said. "I don't know what is going on here, but I'm no hired gunman. If I stand and fight, it's because of principles, not for the money. I spent years being a lawman when it was about the lowest paying job on the frontier."

The judge said, "Forgive my daughter. I can tell that she has offended you, Clint. Of course money is not the primary reason you would help us! And, as she implied but did not come right out and tell you, all of this"—he circled his hand above his head to include the room—"all of this no longer belongs to us. We try to keep up appearances, but...."

"Father," Judy said. "Appearances be damned!"

"Judy!" the judge exclaimed. "Mind your manners. If not for my sake, then for your dear departed mother's."

"I'm sorry," Judy said, not looking sorry at all. "But what importance are appearances when you may be murdered by the Corbett brothers any day now!"

The judge inhaled the cigar and blew smoke into the air. "I'm an old man, my dear. Death does not greatly concern me. You are all that matters to me now."

Clint had heard enough. "Judge," he began, "I think all this talk of dying and the Corbetts is a little out of place. They're just men and there are only two of them. I'll protect you and the town and I'll do it without payment because I want to do it. So let's quit getting upset, and enjoy the morning. When I leave here I'll tell Mayor Beamon my decision, and when the Corbetts arrive I'll take care of them however I must."

"You will have to kill them all," Judy said. "And they might well bring their entire family."

Clint blinked. "No one had said anything about a family of Corbetts. How many might that be?"

"Perhaps twenty."

Clint swallowed and tried to keep his face impassive. Two Corbetts were no big deal, twenty were another matter entirely.

The judge must have read his mind. "I would not think more that a handful would come to Union City. To begin with, I am not dangerous or worth much trouble. They will be expecting Sheriff Houser, not the Gunsmith. Few of the family will come."

"Father, if Clint kills Harry and Williard Corbett, the whole family will come to wipe him out."

Clint sucked on his cigar and studied the floor. "Maybe," he said quietly, "it's time I ought to hear the full story about the Corbetts—right from the beginning."

The judge shrugged as if the Corbetts were of no great importance to him—a rather odd reaction from a man who was about to be killed by that very same family.

"The Corbett family is, was, and forever shall be, white trash, Clint. We had that kind in Tennessee, and they were usually the Northern carpetbaggers who came down to plunder us in the misery of our gallant defeat."

"I see. Where do they live?" Clint was not anxious to rehash the terrible Civil War and its tragic aftermath in the

Deep South. He could see that the judge would like nothing better than to vent his spleen on the subject.

"They live somewhere far to the south of here," Judy said. "And they are the scourge of the Mexican border. A tougher, more vile family has never lived in our New Mexico Territory."

The judge nodded in agreement. "I suppose that the sheriff in El Paso might have a better idea exactly how many of the varmints there are, but I have heard anywhere from fifteen to twenty-five men. Some, of course, are probably distant kinfolk, others counted might just be hired hands who work for the Corbett Ranch along the border."

"That's a hard country down there," Clint said. "One still ruled by the Apache in many areas."

"I am very aware of that," the judge said, glancing at his daughter with a knowing look. A look that said there was some kind of secret knowledge between them concerning the entire subject of the border and its feared and unconquerable Apache.

Clint had trained himself well to read such glances, for they could alert a lawman's suspicions and help him do his job. But now, he was not interested in the subject of Apache, but rather, the Corbett brothers.

"Judge, when were they released from prison?"

"A week ago." The judge studied his cigar. "Exactly ten years to the day that they were caught after murdering old Sheriff Wagoner. They shot the poor old man down while he was napping in his chair. Then they tried to rob the bank and would have succeeded if they hadn't been too drunk to climb onto their horses. I and a number of other citizens were able to apprehend them."

"They should have been hung!"

"I ordered them hung," the judge responded bitterly. "My sentence was overruled by the Governor of the Territory. Naturally, I demanded an explanation."

"And he said?"

"Clint, he said that if my orders to hang Harry and Williard were carried out, then I would be ordering my own death sentence."

Miss Judy touched her father's cheek. "My mother had a very delicate heart condition. The strain of . . . well, Clint, if Father had insisted on the hanging, it would have taken my dear mother's life prematurely. I was just a child, but I understood and begged him not to hang the Corbetts. I wanted both of my parents to live."

"A pretty normal reaction," Clint said.

"Of course it was, but a mistake, I fear," the judge said. "It might have gained a few years of life for your mother, but she knew as well as I that the Corbetts had vowed to kill me when they got out of prison. That knowledge hastened her death."

The judge shook his head with sadness, and it was clear he had suffered much. "All these years living under the shadow of impending death have taken their toll on my own health, Clint. It is true that the coward dies a thousand deaths, the brave man but one. I should have hung those boys, and that is why I no longer fear their return. Living under a death sentence for ten years isn't living—it's just waiting to die."

Now Clint thought he understood the judge's curiously detached attitude about the Corbett brothers. Addison Monroe had made his peace and was ready to die.

The judge said, "Several years ago I mortgaged all that I owned for Judy's mother. There were medical treatments that promised some hope of prolonging her life. The poor woman visited every heart specialist on every continent of the world, and their worthless treatments were tremendously expensive. That is why even the roof over my own head is not mine any longer. I have nothing of real value except honor, these books, a few blooded horses, and my daughter. It is enough for me, but I worry for Judy's future."

"Please stop worrying, Father. You have taught me something about courage and independence."

The judge patted his daughter's hand. "Of course I have. Now that the famous Gunsmith has agreed to help us, I can rest easy, perhaps even sleep again."

Clint looked away for a moment. He had not realized how close these two were and how much his own ability figured into the scheme of things in saving Judge Addison Monroe's life and preserving the happiness of his pretty daughter.

"I have to say something," Clint began. "I can usually handle a couple of outlaws, maybe three or four if they are not too cunning or fast on the draw. But if the Corbetts arrive in Union City with ten or twenty men, I can't possibly protect your life. I'm just one man. My advice would be to disappear for a while."

"I can't," the judge said, "and my daughter won't leave my side, though I've begged and threatened."

"Why can't you go?" Clint asked.

"Because of your 'citizen's arrest' as you called it. And you made an elegant plea for justice. Judy and I applauded your courage. Can you really imagine that we could do that and then run away from trouble?"

Clint looked at the old southern gentleman. Of course Judge Addison Monroe could not run. Ten years ago, at the urging of his wife and only child, he had succumbed to compromising his honor by overturning a just death sentence imposed upon Harry and Williard. The judge had regretted it and been paying for that compromise ever since.

"No," Clint said, "I realize now that you could never run. Not even for a little while. But I want you and Miss

Judy to know that I am capable of failure. In this case, it could cost you both your lives."

"We'll take that chance, Clint," Miss Judy said. "And you honor us with your friendship."

Clint looked into her green eyes. She was a real southern beauty, and he wondered if she had ever been . . . no, of course not. Well, had she even been kissed yet? She looked to be in her early twenties. Even a southern belle must have kissed a few men by that age.

She distracted him with her cool beauty. There was none of the raw animal power of Lotta Cooper, but he had the feeling this girl could be thawed out pretty fast under the right circumstances. But he would not be the man to do it.

The judge coughed and then snubbed out his cigar. "They don't agree with me as well as they used to," he explained.

"When will the trial begin?" Clint asked.

"Tomorrow, God willing."

Clint understood that meant it would start if the Corbetts didn't arrive first.

"Clint," the judge said, "it is my understanding that you and Miss Cooper are the only victims and witnesses. Is that correct?"

"It is."

"Then you and she will have to take the stand and explain the entire circumstances."

Clint glanced at Miss Judy, who looked away quickly. It suddenly occurred to him that spilling out the juicy details to a courtroom of snickering people was not going to be very enjoyable. The hell with them! he thought. To protect Lotta from all the snide and ribald remarks I will lie on the witness stand.

"Judge, we went out to Soldier Creek to do some frogging."

The judge's eyebrows arched up in question. "Frogging?"

"That's right." Clint winked. "Surely, coming from the South, you must remember how tasty frog legs can be?"

The judge smiled and relaxed. "Why, yes! I sure do. And the next time you go 'frogging' with a beautiful woman, I'd like to buy any extra you might have to sell."

"It's a deal." Clint finished his cigar and stood up to take his leave.

The judge knew full well that he and Miss Cooper hadn't been frogging. But he approved of the lie and that Clint would protect Lotta's name from slander by using it.

Miss Judy showed Clint to the door. "I'm glad you are our friend," she said, offering him her hand. "I almost feel we can get through all of this now."

Clint nodded. Standing on the porch of this fine house that did not belong to the judge and his daughter sort of saddened him. He wondered how Miss Judy would make out if the judge were killed. He could not visualize her working in a café or dancehall.

"Clint?"

"Yes."

"You were . . . you weren't really frogging with the woman."

It was not a question and he chose not to lie to her. "No," he said.

"That's what I thought. She is very . . . very beautiful, isn't she?"

"Yes."

"Will she be in my father's courtroom tomorrow?"

"I think that she'll have to be, although she has a miserable cold and would prefer to remain in her sickbed."

"I see. Good-bye, Clint."

He watched her go back inside, and in her long flowing

dress that swept the floor, she seemed so graceful that she glided rather than walked.

"Now, there," he said, wanting what he saw but knowing he would never have the chance to know her intimately because their worlds were so very different, "goes a real lady."

# SEVEN

Clint swung the cell door open, unholstered his sixgun and said, "I couldn't find any handcuffs, so I want you to lie facedown on the floor of my office, side by side."

"What are you goin' to do to us?" the giant, Abe Holoran, rumbled.

"Rope you leg to leg so you can't run."

"Go to hell!"

Clint cocked the hammer of his gun back and said, "I guess you boys know I was a sheriff for a lot of years. Whenever I had prisoners like you, I'd just shoot them and claim they were trying to escape. Maybe that would save us a lot of trouble."

"You ain't doin' that to us!" Abe swore, backing into the cell until he came to the wall.

"I will if I have to. It's up to you."

The three men made up their minds in a hurry and came out and did as they were told. Once they were down, Clint tied their hands behind their backs and then yoked them together at the ankles. They wouldn't be going anywhere now.

"All right," he said, "on your feet and out the door. The judge is waiting."

"For a bullet," the handsome one whose name was Bob Nash said. "The Corbetts will ventilate that old bastard, and then they'll come to free us."

"I'll be around to see it doesn't happen," Clint said. "Now on your feet and start walking."

It was a fine morning. Clear and brisk without a cloud in the sky. With a day as nice as this it was hard to believe that death was riding fast horses straight for Union City.

"Good morning, Clint, darling," Lotta said happily as she sashayed in to walk along behind the prisoners.

"You look pretty well recovered," Clint said, noticing how the color was starting to come back into her cheeks and how her eyes had lost their momentary dullness.

"I am," she said. "But I wish we did not have to go through all this business of a trial. They're guilty as could be, Clint! Why can't the judge just send them off to prison and be done with it?"

"He has to hear their testimony and ours. There has to be some effort to give these three snakes a defense."

"You let *me* have that sixgun you're holding, and I'll give them all the defense they deserve!"

The three men looked around nervously and showed surprising speed considering their legs were roped together.

When they reached the courtroom, the place was filled to capacity and not even a thin cat could have found a seat on one of the hard wooden benches. Miss Judy Monroe was sitting up close to the front and motioned them to come join her, for she had saved them seats.

"She wants *me* to sit with her?" Lotta asked in disbelief.

"Of course. We are the entire prosecution. We have to be up front."

"Mighta known she didn't want to chat with a dancehall singer."

Clint smiled. Lotta pretended that she did not give a damn about what anyone else thought, but this proved her feelings could be just as sensitive as anyone's.

The crowd parted for them, and people stopped talking as they stared at Lotta's plunging neckline and radiant smile. The old respectable women from the town looked down their noses with disapproval, but the old respectable men and all the others with them liked what they saw and stared with unconcealed admiration.

Clint got the three prisoners in their chairs up on the dais and Phil Croker, whom Clint had paid five dollars, covered them from behind with a double-barreled shotgun. Phil looked so worried Clint wondered if he might accidentally pull the trigger and blow the heads off all three prisoners. That would not be so tragic.

"Hear ye. Hear ye. This court is now in session," Croker trilled. The Judge Addison Wetlock Monroe is presiding. Everyone wearin' a hat take it off, and you-all stand up for the judge and stay standin' until he is seated."

The judge came in and everyone stood and the judge banged his gavel down and said, "You may all be seated. This court is now in session. How do you three men plead to the charge of attempted murder?"

Bob Nash, who had apparently been elected the spokesman, said, "Not guilty, Judge. We was only. . . ."

The judge banged his gavel down hard, for he was clearly annoyed. "Save your testimony for after you are sworn in."

Nash colored with embarrassment. "This whole thing is a joke," he said brazenly. "We ain't going to no prison. But you and the Gunsmith are goin' to Boot Hill!"

The courtroom erupted in a chorus of voices, and the

judge had to bang his gavel for almost five minutes before order was restored, and by then he was really mad.

"If there is another outburst like this in my courtroom again, I will run everyone out of here except those that are directly involved in this trial! Is that clearly understood by you-all?"

The spectators nodded and avoided the judge's angry look. There was no doubt that he would do exactly as he threatened.

"First the prosecution," the judge said. "Mr. Clinton Adams, please raise your right hand and repeat after me. Do you, Clinton Adams, agree to tell the truth, the whole truth, and nothing but the truth?"

"I do."

"Then please begin."

Clint began by telling the judge about the trouble his three prisoners had given Miss Lotta in the Bulldog Saloon and how Abe Holoran had even tried to rape her right on the stage.

Some of the male spectators grinned and snickered among themselves but the judge had such a mean glare that they hushed up right away. Clint went on to describe the ride out to Soldier Creek and the events that took place after the three men arrived and began shooting.

"Anything else?" the judge asked.

"Nope. We were just minding our own business and doing a little froggin' when. . . ."

Abe Holoran yelled, "Froggin'! Judge, they weren't froggin'! They was fuckin'!"

The room exploded in a riot of noise. Lotta turned pale, and in two bounds Clint was off the witness stand and bringing his pistol crashing down across Abe's thick skull. The giant pitched forward and struck the floor.

"Bailiff!" the judge roared, banging his gavel over and over and shouting for silence. "Bailiff, gag that man."

"It won't be necessary, Your Honor. Mister Adams knocked him out cold."

"Good!" Judge Monroe said. "And now I order this court cleared. This is not a sideshow for sexual titillation. Bailiff, clear the courtroom at once!"

Miss Judy Monroe had to leave, too, though it was clear she wanted to remain. As she passed Clint, she said, "My father will wrap this up very quickly once the courtroom is empty. I have rarely seen him so furious. My sincerest apologies to Miss Cooper for the embarrassment caused by such uncouth behavior. In my mother's day, such behavior alone before ladies would demand those three be hung."

She went outside and when the last spectator was shoved out the front door, the judge ordered all the doors locked and the windows curtained from prying eyes. He came back and took his place on the bench. "I find you guilty as charged," he said quietly. "And I sentence you each to ten years in the territorial prison. If attempted rape and murder were capital offenses, I would order you all to hang."

"Ten years!" Bob Nash spat on the floor with defiance and disgust. "We won't be in jail ten minutes. You're a dead man, Judge. Dead!"

"Get them back to jail, Gunsmith. I have already wired the Territorial Marshal to come and take them. He should be here in three days."

The Corbetts arrived two days later. Clint was in his office doing some gunsmithing when a rider came pounding up the main street of town, shouting that the Corbetts were on their way.

The three prisoners began to hoot and shout with mirth. "Told you they'd be here to settle the score!" Nash said.

"I want to see them shoot you in the belly so you die

slow," Abe said, the knot on his forehead still ugly and as large as a duck egg.

Clint grabbed an extra pistol that he had been working on and shoved it into his waistband. He picked up his own Winchester rifle and headed for the door in time to see the street emptying as men scattered for safety.

The Gunsmith had asked the town for its help and support. He'd asked, but help wasn't coming. The miners had no stake in this fight and the merchants were all family men who had begged off on account of their responsibilities. But now, there were two jarring surprises. With a brace of old cap-and-ball matched dueling pistols, Judge Monroe stepped out to join Clint, and beside him was his daughter, who was carrying a pretty little shotgun.

"Are you two crazy!" Clint yelled. "Get out of here and let me handle this."

"I can't and she won't."

"That's right!" Judy said tightly. "During the Civil War, the women were not afraid to fight to protect their families and their land. And I am a good shot with either pistol or rifle."

"That's a bird gun!" Clint said.

"Then I'll use this, sir!"

Judy pulled a sixgun out from her handbag. She spun the cylinder, and the gun looked huge in her small fist. "I can hit what I aim for," she said.

From above, a strong voice called, "And so can I!"

They all looked up to see Miss Lotta with a rifle in her hands. She was standing by her window, framed by its lacy curtains.

Clint swore. "Listen, please! This is a gunfight. You'll get yourselves killed if you don't. . . ."

"Gunsmith, I damn sure ain't letting them kill you and neither are they," Lotta said. "So you might as well hold your breath and save it for the Corbett brothers."

Clint looked at all three of them and realized it was

futile to argue. They weren't leaving and there was no chance of changing their minds. So he squared his shoulders and said, "Thanks. Judge, you and your daughter must have had advance warning, because you were ready and waiting."

"We did."

"Mind telling me how many men are about to burst around that corner and come in shooting?"

The judge took a deep breath and said, "I was told to expect an even dozen."

Clint said nothing. He just turned and laid his Winchester down behind him and drew that second pistol from behind his belt. He let it dangle at his left side so when the one in his holster was emptied, he would switch so fast that there would hardly be a break in his firing. Two pistols, twelve bullets plus whatever the women and old Judge Monroe could unleash.

The numbers would work out just fine, unless the Corbetts decided they might like to return fire. In that case, twelve men could fire off sixty or seventy rounds in about five seconds.

Considering it that way, the numbers didn't sound so good anymore. Not good at all.

# EIGHT

Clint was hoping that a way could be found to settle things with the Corbett family in a peaceable manner. He didn't expect that to happen, but it never hurt to extend the olive branch no matter how poor the chances of avoiding bloodshed might seem. There had been many occasions in his long and illustrious law career when a simple way out given to a desperate man had been all that was required. Something like, "Don't you think a jail sentence with a fair chance of parole would be a whole lot better than a bullet and a cold grave with no chance of rising from the dead?"

Usually, when he had phrased it like that and in a reasonable tone of voice, the man Clint was facing would see the light. However, there were two instances where persuasive tactics were likely to fail. They were when the man Clint faced knew that he was going to be hung, and also when Clint found himself greatly outnumbered and outgunned.

Unfortunately, this fell into the latter case.

"Here they come," Clint said, hearing the drum of their horses' hooves. Clint stepped out into the street. "Judge, you and Miss Judy stay on the boardwalk back in the shadows where they won't see you at first. If bullets start flying, I want you both to get the hell inside a building and then start shooting from cover. You'll be no help to anyone if you're caught in the first volley."

"What about me?" Lotta called down to the street.

Clint had half a mind to tell her to remove her blouse and stand right in the open window. With that kind of distraction, he'd even up the odds considerably.

Instead, the Gunsmith called up to her, "Stay out of sight and don't fire a shot unless I open fire first."

Lotta disappeared behind the lace curtains, but the barrel of her rifle was still poking through the window. Clint was about to yell for her to pull it inside the room, but he had run out of time.

A body of fighting men rounded the corner on sweaty horses and came galloping down the Main Street. They were all big, hard-looking riders, and Clint felt a tickle of fear along his backbone as he stood to block their path. The shiny sheriff's badge glinted on his chest, and the thumb of his right hand was hooked into his cartridge belt. They might listen to him, and they might take him out in a single volley. He was about to find out.

The Corbetts drew their horses in, and the huge cloud of dust that followed them rolled down the street and stung Clint's eyes.

"I'm Harry Corbett," the leader said, "and this man right beside me is Williard Corbett. What happened to Sheriff Houser?"

"He ran," Clint said. "I'm taking his place."

"You're fixin' to get shot is what you are doin'," Williard growled.

They were a tall family of men; Williard was nearly

six-and-a-half feet. They were dusty, unshaven, and lean. They were about what you would expect of a family of outlaws who had ridden a couple hundred miles up from the Mexican border with vengeance in their hearts.

"If I die, so do three or four of you," Clint said matter-of-factly. "You should also be aware that I am known as the Gunsmith. I tell you that because, before you choose to die foolishly, you ought to know the name of the man that killed you."

"You're the Gunsmith?" Harry asked.

"He is for a fact," one of the riders behind them said. "I saw him gun down the Tinglehoff Gang in El Paso last year. You and Williard together can't match his speed. Nobody can."

Harry and Williard exchanged worried glances. They had expected to find Houser in hiding. Instead, they faced a legend who looked very determined and absolutely fearless.

"We don't want no fight with you, Gunsmith. It's Judge Monroe that we come to even the score with."

"That's what I've heard. But he only carried out the law. You killed a man and you paid for your crime. At this moment, you boys and the law are squared up even. So why not turn around and ride back to the border before you get right back into deep trouble with the law."

"And you're the new law of Union City," Harry said, looking around the town and deciding that Clint wasn't being backed up by anyone. "Seems to me that a famous man such as yourself could find a better town to die in than this one. Hell, nobody else has even got the guts to stand with you."

"I do," Judge Monroe shouted as he stepped out of the shadows with Miss Judy trying to pull him back and failing.

"Damn!" Clint swore softly.

The judge had a dueling pistol gripped in each of his bony fists. "I am at your service," he said with a smile and a formal bow of his head. "And I see that prison has not taught either of you wisdom. You should have been hanged ten years ago."

Clint groaned. The judge had disobeyed his orders and his timing could not have been worse. Given half a chance, Clint had begun to believe he might have turned the Corbetts back. But now, as Harry and Williard twisted in their saddles to see the man that they blamed for their recent years of hell, Clint saw that the chance for peaceful negotiations was lost.

Insane with hatred, Harry and Williard went for their guns. Clint shot Harry before the man cleared his holster, but Williard surprised him by diving off his horse. He struck the ground, and his horse reared, momentarily blocking a clear shot by the Gunsmith. Clint saw Williard rolling in the thick dust. He saw men clawing for their sixguns. The Gunsmith threw himself behind a heavy watering trough that he had planned on using from the very beginning if hell started popping.

Clint came up firing at the riders. A man screamed and tumbled out of the saddle, but his boot caught in the stirrup. Man and horse went plunging through the other horsemen, creating sheer havoc. The dust and the bullets were flying so thickly that Clint was almost afraid to shoot for fear his bullets might crash through storefronts and kill innocent men across the street.

He heard Lotta's Winchester open up from above and then the whoosh-bang of the judge's old black powder dueling pistols. He thought he heard Miss Judy scream, but the bullets were flying so thick that he dared not try to help her. So instead, he emptied his sixgun and then used the spare. Men were being hit and hit hard. With the bite of gunsmoke in his nostrils, the Gunsmith saw them being slammed out of their saddles or else suddenly slump over the necks of their horses, which were plunging in fear and ruining their aim.

We're going to win this, Clint thought grimly. If they'd been smart enough to dismount and shoot from behind cover, we would not have stood a chance. But they stayed together on horseback and . . .

He heard Lotta yelp once and then twisted around to see her pitch forward out of her window. She did a complete somersault on the way down and crashed through the porch roof of Amos Avery's Emporium. Clint came to his feet running and firing, though he knew that Lotta was dead before she hit the boardwalk.

He grabbed her and dragged her body into the store as a swarm of bullets followed in his wake.

She *was* dead. Shot through that brave heart of hers. Clint looked up with tears in his eyes. He saw Avery crouching behind his counter with fear.

"Get me a loaded shotgun!" the Gunsmith shouted as he punched the shells out of his gun and reloaded.

"I got one ready!"

Holstering his loaded sixgun, Clint ran over and yanked it from the frightened man's fist. It was new and it was double-barreled. Clint whirled and raced for the door. He threw himself outside in a rolling dive that carried him completely over the boardwalk into the street. And when he stopped rolling, he raised the shotgun and blew the hell out of the Corbett gang, those that were still alive in their saddles.

The twin blasts from the big twelve-gauge broke the gang as if they were just a handful of twigs. Clint dropped the shotgun and fired at the last three Corbetts. His bullet knocked a Corbett off his horse, and the man did not move after he stopped rolling in the dust. The other two were hit as they struggled to stay in their saddles, for they were badly wounded. They reined away and spurred down the street, furiously trying to escape with their lives. Clint could have killed them before they rounded the corner at the edge of town and vanished, but he had never shot a man in the back before and he could not start now.

So he holstered his sixgun and walked back into the emporium. He picked up Lotta Cooper and carried her down the street to where Miss Judy was standing with tears funneling down her pale cheeks.

"Father is dying," she said. "He took a bullet in the lungs."

Clint placed Lotta down carefully and smoothed her hair. "I'll go get the doctor," he said.

"No, he wants to talk to you before he dies. It's . . . it's too late for a doctor, Clint. I know that and so does my father. I'll stay here beside Miss Cooper."

Clint swallowed noisily. "Thanks," he said. He walked over to the judge and saw that Miss Judy had called it right. The old Southerner was failing rapidly but when he opened his eyes to see the Gunsmith, he smiled.

"Did you get them?" he asked.

"Yeah. All but two and they were winged bad. I don't think we'll ever hear from the Corbett family again."

"Good!" The judge smiled, though the rest of his face was a mask of pain. "Mr. Adams," he wheezed as bloody froth edged the corners of his mouth, "you should have seen the way my daughter stood and fought! It was the proudest moment of my life. She's . . . she's a Tennessee Monroe if there ever was one."

"Let me go get her. She should be with you now."

"Hear me out first, sir. I . . . I want you to take her down into the wilds of southeastern Arizona. To. . . ."

His eyes fluttered and his frail old body shuddered.

"Judy!" Clint called. "Come quick!"

The girl raced over to her father and held his hand to her bosom.

"My dear girl," the judge said, "you look like an angel."

"I'm not, Father. I just want you to live!"

"You know that is impossible, my dear. Besides, I have lived well and long. It is time that I joined your dear mother, and I thank God that I die fighting and in honor rather than wasting away in my bed."

The judge smiled and turned his eyes back to Clint. "Mr. Adams, I want you to take my daughter to find the Lost Apache Mine down in the—" He coughed and it was a terrible sight and sound. When he finally caught his breath, he gasped, "Down in the Chiricahua Mountains."

"Sir . . . that's too dangerous a country to take your daughter into!"

"Then I beg you—go without her. She . . . she has the map given to her by her Uncle Moses Malone. He gave it to her on his deathbed and swore to its validity."

Clint nodded but thought it very sad that the judge would be wasting his last ounce of strength telling him about a mine that everyone knew had never existed except in someone's ripe imagination.

Clint was familiar with the Chiricahuas. They were the last Apache stronghold in the United States and a no-man's-land where even the Army feared to go.

"Mr. Adams," the judge whispered, his voice like sandpaper, his eyes shrunk far back into his head. "I am no fool! I know what you are thinking and you are . . . wrong! The Lost Apache Mine really exists! My brother saw it with his own. . . ."

The judge could not continue. With the last of his strength, he grabbed Clint's wrist and said, "Promise me you'll help my daughter. It's all I have left to give . . . her!"

He coughed terribly and when the rattle died in his

throat, he was dead. Judy fell across his chest and wept piteously.

Clint left her to walk slowly back to Lotta Cooper. He picked the woman up and headed for the livery stable to rent a team of horses, a buckboard, and a shovel. The townspeople had begun to filter back into the street. They were wide-eyed with excitement and stared at the dead Corbetts, who littered the battle-torn street.

Clint ignored everyone. He was taking Lotta for a drive in the buckboard, and he was going to bury her in the little meadow where they had made love so often. It was funny, but Lotta might have sensed her own impending death. She had given Clint specific instructions where she wanted to be buried.

No gawking crowds. No pious eulogy, because she had never been a churchgoer. Just the green meadow, the cobalt sky, and Soldier Creek to babble softly to her in the night.

The Gunsmith would give her those things, and he would give her his grief.

# NINE

A knock at his door turned the Gunsmith away from packing his clothes in an old canvas warbag he tied behind his saddle. Since Lotta Cooper's death, Union City held no charm for him anymore, and he had decided to leave. There was a woman waiting for him in Santa Fe, and he needed a shoulder to cry on for a while. Losing Lotta had hit him harder than he might have expected.

"Who is it?"

"It's Judy. Miss Judy Monroe."

Clint unlocked his door and said, "I was under the impression it was not proper for a young woman to come up to a man's room unescorted."

His words were spoken with a smile, and they did what he had hoped they might—they completely disarmed his visitor.

"You smiled," Clint said.

Judy Monroe shrugged. "I didn't think I'd be capable of that for a long, long time. May I come in?"

"Sure." He stepped aside and let her enter, but he left the door open. He didn't want to leave any wagging tongues in this town.

"Mr. Adams, you're leaving." It was not a question and it was said sharply. "After promising my father that you would take me to the Chiracahua Mountains to find our Lost Apache Mine, you're sneaking off without even a good-bye."

Clint stiffened as if he had been slapped in the face. "I never promised your father anything. He asked me to take you, I told him it was too dangerous. I was right then, and I'm still right."

"So you're just leaving."

"Correct." Clint looked at the girl, and he could tell she was on the verge of tears. She was dressed in black, and her face had lost flesh so that she looked hollow-cheeked and very wan. "I'm sorry I didn't attend your father's funeral. I watched the procession from that window, and there was a big crowd of mourners. I figured that, among all those people, my presence would not be missed."

Her dark eyes flashed. "It was badly missed, sir. *You* counted, not them. Where were they when my father needed them! Where were they when you, I, Miss Cooper, and my father stood before the Corbetts!"

Clint was surprised at the vehemence in her voice. He did not blame her at all, but he was surprised. "You have to forgive them," he said. "Their lack of . . . of gumption was not unusual. I've sheriffed for dozens of towns, and I learned a long time ago that you can't ever count on the everyday citizen to stand up and fight. That's supposed to be the lawman's job. That's what they pay him to do."

"I despise them!" Judy said angrily. "My father was their judge for almost ten years, and he belonged to all their cozy civic clubs, their lofty little organizations. And when it came time to repay him by standing at his side, he found them all wanting . . . except a gunsmith and a . . . a woman who danced in a saloon."

"And his daughter," Clint reminded softly. "He didn't die a bitter man, Judy. You should forgive just as he did."

Judy lifted her skirts and sat down on the Gunsmith's bed. She smoothed her dress and was silent for a moment, then said, "Where are you going now?"

"South, I think. Maybe to Santa Fe for the rest of the summer."

"I'm going to the Chiricahua Mountains," she told him. "I have sold everything we own that was not of sentimental value, and I am looking for someone to lead me to the Lost Apache Mine."

Clint shook his head sadly. "That's a fool's. . . ." He saw fierce anger blaze in her eyes, and he modified his words.

"Miss Judy," he began, choosing what he had to say with great care, "I have been all through the Chiricahuas and am considered very lucky to be alive and yet very foolish for taking the risk in the first place. But sometimes, the men I tracked were so desperate they would ride anywhere to escape the reach of the law. Those are bad mountains: hard, mostly dry, and big. Only the Apache and the outlaws who trade with them travel in that land."

"Mr. Adams, I know the risks. My Uncle Moses died as the result of an arrow wound that became infected. It was a lingering, tragic death. Sometimes, he was delirious. He spoke of the Chiricahuas constantly and never with any fondness."

"Then. . . ."

"Let me finish, please. When someone is delirious and dying, they are incapable of lying. They may hallucinate, but they have not the ability to lie. My uncle talked about the Lost Apache Mine with the conviction of a man who has been there and escaped. He took three nuggets, and the Apache caught and tortured him for two days and nights.

They broke his health, but he still escaped to return to us and die. And he still had the three nuggets."

Judy looked right into his eyes. "I have one left, Mr. Adams. Would you like to see it?"

Despite himself, he found he was nodding his head.

She removed a huge nugget from her purse and laid it in the palm of his outstretched hand. It was the size of a robin's egg, and it had been beaten smooth by Indians. Even in the poor light of his room, Clint could see the words scratched in gold. Lost Apache Mine—AZ.

"Now what do you think?" she asked him softly.

He gave the big gold nugget back to her. "I don't think gold is worth life," he said. "The nuggets could have come from anywhere in the West. And anywhere in the West would be safer than the Chiricahuas."

She sighed and shook her head. "You have nothing to prove to me, Mr. Adams. You are the bravest man I have ever known. Good-bye and good luck to you, sir."

She eased off the bed and started to leave, but he called her back. "Miss Judy, don't go into those mountains!"

"I have to go," she said, halting at his door. "My uncle died for that mine, and my father died believing that he had not left me without a means of subsistence."

She smiled almost whimsically. "But it isn't just the money, Mr. Adams. It's . . . it's become a matter of family honor. If I did not try to find it, then I would hate myself for the rest of my life. And I would wonder if I could have found it had I the courage and the heart."

"It isn't there," he said. "Listen . . . it just does not exist!"

"We shall see. I have two good men who are eager to help me locate that mine—for equal shares. I intend to hire them right now and leave today."

"Equal shares! You mean they each want a third?"

"That's right."

"That's *way* too much," Clint snapped. "It was your uncle who found the damn thing, and you're financing the expedition. Offer them fifty percent, take it or leave it."

But Judy shook her head. "They won't take it."

"Then tell them to go . . . go jump in Soldier Creek," Clint said lamely.

"I can't. You've refused me so I have no other alternatives. My back is to the wall."

Clint scowled and scrubbed his jaw. "Who are these two 'good men' you're going to hire?"

"Shorty Blevins and Vince Hacken."

"Shorty and Vince are going to lead you into the Chiracahuas!" Clint barked a laugh of derision. "Those boys have never been more than fifty miles from Union City. They've never even seen an Apache, and they'll get you killed!"

"At least they are willing to try. No one else is, that's for sure." She stuck out her hand and Clint took it. "Goodbye, Mr. Adams. And I hope you enjoy your stay in Santa Fe. I'm sure that you will."

"When were you supposed to leave?" Clint growled, thoroughly upset about the fact that two fools like Shorty and Vince would presume to take a lady into such danger. They must have been half-drunk when they agreed to the deal and when they sobered up, they'd back down from their offer.

"We *are* leaving, Mr. Adams. And it will be within the hour. Shorty and Vince said they would buy what was needed, and all I have to do is pay the bills and saddle my horse."

Clint groaned. "You've given those two fools a blank check for a disaster," he said in a flat, uncompromising voice. "They'll buy things you don't need and forget things you do need."

Judy Monroe's chin snapped up, and her voice took on an edge of anger. "That really is of no concern to you, is it? I have asked, almost begged, you to lead me into the Chiricahuas. You have flatly refused. I have no other alternatives and I will not give up."

"Shorty and Vince will sober up within ten miles of here, and I don't trust them not to leave you stranded on foot. They'll be back before dark."

"Don't count on it!"

She whirled and stomped away, leaving the Gunsmith standing alone in his room. He began to pace up and down, glancing out at the street every few minutes. True to her promise, he saw Miss Judy and those two fools she had hired go riding by. Vince and Shorty were a couple of ex-miners, ex-cowboys, and ex-everything else, who had failed at every job and occupation they'd ever attempted. Neither man had any sense of commitment to a profession. They were sleazy little opportunists who were now waving to all the townspeople and yelling about how they were going to come back rich.

The sight of those two made Clint want to vomit. They didn't deserve to be with Miss Judy, and he knew they would rob her and leave her stranded somewhere.

I should go after her, he thought. But if they sober up as fast as I expect they will and desert her, she'll come back and give up that fool notion of the Lost Apache Mine. So I'll wait. 'Cause if I go after her now, then she wins and I've lost out to her game, and we will both ride into the Apache hell.

Clint turned away from the window and headed for the nearest saloon. He would wait for Miss Judy there and when she returned, he would even give her a little comfort and sympathy.

Darkness found the Gunsmith with more whiskey in his belly than he had intended to drink. Even worse, Miss Judy and her two idiot guides were still gone.

They'll be camped less than fifteen miles from here, he thought, then they'll come straggling in tomorrow afternoon with their tails tucked between their legs and their tongues all hairy from whiskey. But I won't say a word about how I told her so. Nope. I'll be sympathetic as hell and a real gentleman, the way the judge would have been.

Clint went up to his room but despite the whiskey, he was too restless to sleep so he propped his boots up on his window sill and watched the street below, just in case Miss Judy came in late in the night.

He awoke on the floor, feeling stiff and with a pain in his skull. He climbed to his feet and splashed cold water on his face from the pitcher and basin on his bedside table.

Clint combed his hair with his fingers and studied himself in the mirror. His eyes were red and he looked awful. He thought about shaving but decided he might cut his own throat. So he dressed, strapped on his gun, and was surprised to see that his hat still fit on his big head. He staggered downstairs and headed for a cafe where they served a hung-over man all the hot coffee he wanted for a nickel. Later, he'd think about food.

He waited all day for the three of them and when they did not return by darkness, the idea finally took hold in the Gunsmith's mind that Shorty and Vince might actually be dumb enough to think they could get into the Chiricahua Mountains and back out alive with the Apaches' gold.

"I will give those fools one more day," he thought, but again, he slept poorly.

When he awoke, he was clearheaded and determined to put a stop to Miss Judy Monroe's madness. He would catch those three and bring them back before they rode any deeper into trouble.

But they had a two-day head start on him now. Clint was worried. Two days of hard riding was a good hundred-mile lead, even for people not accustomed to travel.

Clint packed his belongings again and headed for the emporium where he would buy all the provisions he would need for a long, fast trail south.

He was angry. Angry at Vince and Shorty, but even angrier at himself for waiting so long. It was just possible that those three fools would reach the Chiricahuas before he did. And if that happened, it might be too late to save them from the Apache.

At the livery, he bailed out his big black gelding, Duke. The animal was sleek and his coat shone from regular brushing and graining. Clint saddled the horse and tied his provisions on, behind the cantle of his saddle. He had a good bedroll, a canvas sheet for rain, and enough food to travel light and fast.

He also had plenty of ammunition both for his gun and rifle. Clint mounted the horse, and it felt good to be back in the saddle again.

"You've put on a little weight, the same as me," he told the high-spirited animal. "Well, pardner, I'm afraid we're both going to be a whole lot leaner before we ever get back this way again."

"Where you goin' so early?" the owner of the livery shouted.

"To an Apache hell," he replied, touching Duke with his spurs and galloping on a long trail southwest.

# TEN

Clint rode hard all that first day and when he dropped down out of the Sangre de Cristos, he saw the silver thread of the Rio Grande. It was impossible to know which route the three he followed had taken, and there were far too many hoofprints to pick up their trail. That being the case, he did the only thing he could do and that was to set his own course and trust that he could beat Miss Judy and her two inept guides to the little town of Santa Rosa in the southwestern corner of New Mexico. All trails into the Chiricahua Mountains led through Santa Rosa, and that was where Clint hoped to intercept and save Miss Judy.

As the Gunsmith pushed Duke down the forested mountainside toward the Rio Grande River, he tried not to think about what might happen if he missed the trio or was too late to intercept them before they disappeared. The Chiricahuas were so wild and inhospitable, they could swallow up a company and cavalry as if it had never existed.

Waterholes were hard to find, there were endless box-canyons, and the heat could be unmerciful.

On the second day out of Union City, Clint rode into Albuquerque and stopped for a couple of hours rest. He had Duke grained and given a good brushing and rubdown; the horse was already ganted up in the loins and his coat was thick with salt and dried sweat.

Clint was stiff and sore. It was one thing to ride a horse fast across flatland, quite another to come down from a mountain range. Albuquerque was warm and he was unac-customed to the heat. Well, Clint thought, I had better get accustomed to the heat fast.

Sheriff Jason B. Tringle was cleaning a rifle at his desk when Clint walked into his office. Before he could even introduce himself to the sheriff, the man stood up and said, "Well, I'll be damned, it's the Gunsmith!"

The sheriff, a boyish-looking six-footer, had a wide and friendly smile and he stuck out his hand.

"It's an honor to finally meet you. I saw you gun down Travis Miranda over in Tucumcari about two years ago. I'll never forget how you tried to talk him out of that fight before you killed him."

Clint remembered. "Travis was a hot-head. I wanted to wing him in the shoulder, but he swung sideways when he drew his gun, and my shot took him square in the chest. I felt bad about that killing."

"Then you were the only one in town who did. Travis was not only hot-headed, he was mean. He came from a bad family that has, unfortunately, moved into my county. The whole bunch of them are a thorn in my side. If you hadn't shot Travis, someone else would have, and it would probably have been me. Travis, more than any of the Mir-andas, was out of control."

Clint sympathized, but he was not concerned with the Miranda family anymore. He'd seen them and his judgment was the same as the sheriff's. Bad blood always bred bad blood.

"I've come by to ask if you've seen a pretty, dark-haired woman on a Thoroughbred horse come riding through town in the last twenty-four hours. "She'd be escorted by two men in their thirties, both smallish, both disreputable-looking with full beards. They also brag a lot in the saloons."

Sheriff Tringle shook his head. "Can't say I have. But why don't you and I go ask around in a couple of the saloons?"

"I'd appreciate that," Clint said. "You see, the girl thinks that those two men are qualified to take her into the Chiricahuas. But they aren't. I'm trying to catch and stop them before they get into real trouble."

"Why would anyone go down there into that Apache stronghold?"

"Gold. Miss Judy has a map her uncle gave her of a lost gold mine."

The sheriff groaned. "Not another one."

"Yep."

They headed up one end of town and came back down the other checking at each saloon. Word of the Gunsmith's presence soon spread through Albuquerque and when noon came around, a sizable number of men were following them in and out of the saloons.

Sheriff Tingle shook his head at the crowd following them and said, "Do you always attract this kind of attention?"

"Nope. Only when some fool spreads the word I'm looking for someone. Then everybody expects there will be a gunfight. I was once told that it would be even better if I got killed. Then the ones who saw it could brag that they were there when the Gunsmith finally went down."

They pushed into the last saloon. The sheriff shook his

head in amazement at the throng of curious and excited men who followed them hoping to see a gunbattle involving someone famous. "I never realized that being a living legend could have its drawbacks. I always thought that. . . . Look out!"

Clint whirled, hearing the twin retorts of guns and cursing himself for not paying more attention to what he was doing. He had allowed himself to become mentally lax and distracted by the sheriff's talk. Now, as he drew his gun and dove for the sawdust floor, a bullet ripped through the muscle of his left arm. A second bullet bit into the batwing doors and a third hit the sheriff in the leg and threw him out into the street to writhe in pain.

Clint fired as fast as he could pull the trigger. There was no time to aim, only to react and shoot toward the two muzzle flashes that blinked in the shadows. When his gun was empty, he rolled sideways and knocked a poker table over to use as cover. He punched out the empty shells and reloaded, though he did it clumsily for his left arm was almost useless and a rapid, numbing effect was creeping swiftly into his fingers.

There was no sound from the back of the long, dim saloon, and Clint thought that he had probably killed the two men.

"Throw out your guns!" he yelled, "and stand up with your hands over your head."

There was no answer. Clint got his feet under him and rose slowly. He saw other patrons of the saloon caught in the dangerous crossfire lying flat on the sawdust floor. The bartender's head popped into sight, and the man looked scared.

Clint could not see the two men who had tried to kill him. They were behind an overturned table at the shadowed far end of the room. Suddenly, he heard a floorboard creak in protest, and he spun to his left and fired upward.

His first shot smashed a chandelier and his second dropped a man who had been about to ambush him from the balcony. The man slammed backward through an open door, and Clint knew at a glance that the ambusher was dead.

The Gunsmith turned around in a full circle, with his left arm dangling uselessly at his side and warm blood seeping down his sleeve. He wanted to get to a doctor before he lost too much blood. But first, he asked, "Has anyone here seen a couple of men either yesterday or this morning who were bragging about gold in the Chiricahua Mountains?"

"No, sir!" the bartender said, shaking his head back and forth.

The other patrons of the saloon all shook their heads. Clint expelled a deep breath of disappointment and started to turn. Then he halted and looked back at the bartender. "Who were those three?"

"The Mirandas. You killed one of them a couple of. . . ."

Clint turned away and walked outside to attend to Sheriff Tingle. He didn't need to hear anything more because he knew who he had already killed. He never forgot a single one of the men he had sent to Boot Hill.

Someone had already gone for a doctor, and Sheriff Tingle was up and leaning on a hitching rail. "So, you killed the last of them," he said through gritted teeth. "Thanks for saving my life. They'd have ambushed me sooner or later."

Clint nodded. "I'll wait for the doctor to patch up his arm and then I'll be riding."

Sheriff Tingle studied the wound. "Yours is worse than mine. You need to stay down for a few days. You're in no shape to face the Chiricahuas."

"Neither is Miss Judy Monroe."

The sheriff nodded. "I now know one thing for sure,

walking around with the Gunsmith can be hazardous to a man's health."

Clint tore a strip of his ruined shirt away and allowed a pretty woman to tie it around his torn bicep. "Thank you, ma'am," he said.

She kissed him on the cheek. "Thank you, Mister. For saving my husband's life."

Clint looked to the sheriff who was white with pain. No wonder the man had forgotten to introduce his wife. Now, he wondered, where in blazes is that doctor?

# ELEVEN

The Gunsmith staggered into Santa Rosa, New Mexico in a sea of nausea and pain, feeling weak from the loss of blood and dizzy from the punishing summer heat. Duke had lost a shoe thirty miles north of town on a shortcut across unpopulated country. The gelding had been lame for the last two days. Clint had led his mount all the way in and had been angry at himself for not taking a few hours in Union City to have the horse freshly shod. Because of the loss of time, Clint knew that he had probably failed to overtake Miss Judy and her two inept guides.

As much as he hated to, the Gunsmith knew that he had to rest and heal his wounds before he entered Apache country. He would be of no use to Miss Judy if he passed out in the Chiricahua Mountains or was too weak to defend her or himself. Fortunately, there was a woman in Santa Rosa named Molly Mullane, a red-headed Irisher who owned a small poker-parlor and who could deal cards and play as good a game of poker as anyone that Clint had ever seen.

Molly didn't win all the time, but she won often enough to support herself quite well. She didn't drink and she never cheated. And if you tried to double deal or cheat Molly Mullane at her own table, she just asked you to leave and never return. No threats, no recriminations, no gunplay. Her cool politeness had the effect of making a cheater feel like dirt.

A man who shamefacedly had to exit Molly's Place with his tail between his legs was branded a cheater for life. No one wanted that kind of a reputation. A man might deal off the bottom of a deck around a campfire or in a cabin or in any one of the hundreds of saloons and gambling palaces in the West, but he never cheated at Molly's Place. And because of that, the best gamblers in the country often went out of their way to stop at Santa Rosa to test their skills against Molly and the other professionals.

Molly and Clint went back a number of years and now, as the Gunsmith wobbled dizzily into town, Duke seemed to remember the way almost as well as he did. The weary gelding's ears pricked forward and his head lifted with expectation, because Molly had often given him cubes of sugar or cane syrup on a big ladle.

Clint tied the horse up in front of Molly's Place and was pleased to see that it had not changed a whit since he had been through this way two years before. The gambling parlor was a two-storied house and all the poker was played on the bottom floor. Upstairs, Molly lived with her piano, books, and paintings. Few men had ever been invited upstairs, even fewer spent the night.

Clint took a deep breath and removed his Stetson. He was having trouble with double vision and he leaned against Duke's hitching post until he could see right again. Still feeling woozy and sick, he struggled to bat the dust off his clothes. He figured that if he never walked another step again in his whole life, that would be just fine. The white picket gate swung open with a creaking noise, and he swayed across the stepping stones to the porch.

There was a little bell beside the front door, and although most of Molly's guests probably figured it was brass, the Gunsmith knew very well that it was solid gold. Clint pulled the leather string and the bell tinkled in announcement of his arrival. He heard voices fall silent inside and then he relaxed when he heard Molly say, "You boys hang onto that money and don't move a penny of it until I see who is at my door."

When she came to the door, her hand flew to her mouth, and she cried "As I live and breath! Clint Adams! Come inside and— You've been shot!"

She threw the door open and grabbed him, and she felt mighty comforting. She smelled good, too. Molly had always loved French perfumes and, unlike many women, she knew how to use them so that their fragrance wasn't strong enough to kill flying insects at sixty paces.

"Oh, you look awful!" she exclaimed. "And have you been mistreating Duke as well?"

"Afraid so," Clint said sheepishly. "I didn't have time to stop and bring you a present this time but. . . ."

Suddenly, his legs buckled and he was falling to the porch. He heard Molly shout and then he heard nothing.

He awoke in Molly's bed, and it came as no big surprise that she was in it. He was aware of her cool hands gliding over his loins and then her fingers as they began to tease and play with his flaccid manhood.

Clint smiled because he started to grow hard despite the fact that he felt weak. That was a credit to Molly because, in his current condition, it took some real skill to do what she was doing.

"The doctor said you should remain flat on your back

for a week," Molly said, kissing his chest. "Aren't I the lucky one! I've never before had you captive for so long."

Clint kissed her fragrant hair and slipped his hand over her ample buttocks. Molly was built with a little extra padding but every loving ounce of it was in the right places. She was not perfectly shaped like Lotta Cooper had been, but she used every ounce of herself to pleasure a man, and she could play his twangy fiddle as expertly as she could play poker.

"I can't stay a week," he whispered in her ear.

"You have to," Molly said, climbing up on his now rigid tool and easing herself down on him with a moan of pleasure. He felt himself slip wetly into her slick heat, and he closed his eyes again.

Molly giggled with anticipation. "I may just screw you to death tonight and finish the job someone else couldn't finish."

"I've lost a lot of . . . uhhhh, that feels good. A lot of blood, Molly."

Her hips were moving up and down and then around and around on him, and his toes were curling because she felt so good.

"Molly, I'm a very . . . ohhhh, yeah . . . a very weak man," he protested, kneading her buttocks and pulling her into him so that he was buried in her to the hilt.

"I can tell," she said with a throaty laugh as she pumped him harder and harder. "Even weak, you're a better man in bed than most are healthy. Now stop talking and save your energy for what is important."

Clint smiled. She raised up on her elbows and draped her big breasts in his face, and his lips found her turgid nipples and played with them. Molly began to hump him faster. She had always been easy to arouse through her breasts, and nothing had changed that lovely fact during the past two years. The woman was no raging beauty, but no healthy man would ever kick her out of their bed.

"Hurry, Gunsmith! I'm. . . ."

She began to yelp with ecstasy as her body stiffened and her hips slammed into his harder and harder. Clint clutched her tightly and when he could stand it no longer, he lost control and filled her with his seed. "You haven't changed at all," she said, stroking his flanks. "Still handsome. Still in a big hurry to go somewhere."

"I do have to go somewhere," he told her. "I have to go find and rescue a transplanted southern belle in the Chiricahua Mountains before she is raped and scalped by the Apache."

"Now why would a sweet little 'southern belle' go into those awful mountains alone?"

"I didn't say she was alone," Clint said, "though she might be better off if she was. Two greedy fools from Union City convinced her that they could help her find a lost Apache gold mine."

"And she fell for that old story!" Molly rolled off the Gunsmith and propped her head up on a pillow encased in satin.

"It might not be just another treasure hunt story," Clint said, trying to defend Miss Judy from sounding so stupid as to put her life in danger. "Her uncle actually found the mine and brought out three gold nuggets before he died."

"I don't believe it."

"I saw one," Clint said.

"Darling, you know as well as I do that it might have come from Colorado, California, the Comstock. It could have been prospected anywhere."

Clint did not bother to tell her about the words scratched into its soft surface because that proved nothing. "He gave her a map and he loved her," Clint said. "A man would not give his niece a one-way ticket to a hoax. He must have believed that he had found a fortune."

Molly sat up and looked at the Gunsmith. "It's been my experience that people often start to believe a thing if they want it too much. I've seen that happen lots of times. A person wants something and so they keep thinking about it and it becomes real to them. That's what probably happened, Clint. It was the wantin' that made it real, not the having."

"I still saw that nugget," Clint said. "And anyway, what I think means nothing. It's what the girl thinks that is important. She believes there is a Lost Apache Mine and that she has the map to where it can be found."

"It will be the cause of her death, I fear," Molly said. "She sounds like a fool and therefore is not worth risking your life for."

Clint smiled. "She and her father stood side by side with me against a family called the Corbetts. Her father died trying to help me, and he asked me to find that mine for his daughter."

"And you promised to do it?"

"No," Clint said, "but neither did I tell him I would *not* do it."

"I think you had better forget the southern belle and stay with me awhile. You look hard-used, Clint. You need caring for."

"How about when I come back," he said.

"But you might not come back."

"I'm afraid that's a chance you'll just have to take," the Gunsmith said.

Molly grabbed his manhood again and began to knead it into life.

"What. . . ."

"I decided that as long as you were bound and determined to get yourself killed by the Apache that I might as well go ahead and screw you to death anyway."

Clint laughed. "Take your best shot," he said, lacing his fingers behind his head—but he couldn't keep them there for long.

# TWELVE

Molly scooped a big spoonful of sweet maple syrup from a gallon can and let Duke lick it off. It was the third one he'd lapped up in the space of two minutes, and the Gunsmith just shook his head. "He's sure got a sweet-tooth, don't he," Clint said from atop the big gelding.

"He sure does." Molly placed the lid on the big syrup can and handed it and the ladle up to the Gunsmith.

"I haven't got room to take this!"

"Sure you have," Molly said. "It's imported all the way from Vermont. The finest money can buy, and you really ought to try a little for yourself before giving it all to poor Duke."

Clint knew there was no sense in arguing with Molly. The woman had a stubborn streak as wide as her bouncy backside. "Thanks," he said, hugging it to his belly. "Thanks for everything."

"Just come back," Molly told him, her smiling face suddenly very serious. "The betting odds are now four to one that you won't make it back alive. And that's in my own poker parlor where they know you and don't want to worry me unnecessarily."

Clint just shook his head. He leaned down and stroked Molly's pretty red hair. He liked her freckles and her mischievous green eyes, and he wondered how such an emerald as she had ever wound up in a little border town like Santa Rosa.

"You take those odds for me," he said, pulling forty dollars out of his Levi's and giving it to the woman. "And when I come back, we'll use my winnings to close this place down and go celebrate in El Paso."

Molly grinned, showing a set of fine, white teeth. "That's a good idea as far as it goes. But I think I'll put a hundred dollars of my own money on you. That way, we can go all the way to New Orleans and have a high old time for a couple of months."

"It's a deal," Clint said. "But don't let them put a time limit less than six months on my return. It may take a long while to track Miss Judy down and get her out of there."

"What about the gold mine? If you find it, are you going to bring some back?"

"All I can carry," he promised.

Molly's green eyes danced with excitement at the prospect. "You add a couple of sacks of gold nuggets to our winnings and we could go all the way to Paris, France!"

"Let's keep that in mind." Clint tipped his hat to the lady gambler and rode away with a tight smile on his lips.

He had recuperated in Molly's bed for three days, knowing that he had to build his blood up for the trials he faced in Arizona Territory. Now, he was fit enough to travel and eager to make up for lost time.

Molly had hired a man to make inquiries at every business establishment in Santa Rosa but not one person had seen Miss Judy or her two friends. That meant they must have crossed into Arizona somewhere to the north.

There was a hundred miles of mountains to search and ten thousand things waiting that could kill a man. Besides the Apaches, there were marauding Mexican banditos just as ruthless as the Indians. Clint guessed if Miss Judy had thought for a month she could not have picked a worse place to hunt for gold. And because he vaguely remembered the vicinity of the Lost Apache Mine from the map her uncle had drawn, he felt sure that he would soon find the girl.

As he rode out into the prairie, he wondered what he would do if she still refused to come back to Union City where she belonged.

I will tie her in the saddle and take her by force, he thought. And then I will ride back to Molly in Santa Rosa and collect our winnings.

But since there wasn't any gold there wouldn't be any Paris, France. Still, New Orleans was a stem-winder of a town to have fun in with a girl as lively as Molly Mullane. Maybe they would play a little high stakes strip poker right in the stagecoach on the way to New Orleans!

Clint chuckled. He removed the lid from the can of maple syrup and dipped his finger into the honey-colored stuff. Damn that was good!

Clint scooped out a whole handful, and it was delicious but mighty messy to eat on horseback. He gobbled it up and then sucked his fingers dry before smacking his lips in appreciation. Duke rolled his eyes around toward the back of his head.

"Sorry, fella. If there's any left when we stop to make camp tonight, I'll give you a lick or two. But don't count on it."

The horse flattened his ears with displeasure almost as if he understood what was taking place. But Clint ignored him and rode on toward a rendezvous deep in Apache country. He had been in this land before and survived and he would do so again. His left arm was healing nicely and there was none of the infection that had made him so dizzy when he had led Duke into Santa Rosa.

The trick was to find Miss Judy as fast as possible and be out of the Chiricahuas before they were discovered by the Apache. Because once those devils found you there was no chance of escape. And Apache could travel across a desert faster than most horses. A warrior was trained as a child to run a hundred miles without rest, and he could smell water twenty miles away.

Some of the Plains Indians liked to dress up fancy in beads and bright features. Not the Apache. They wore a few skins, and there was no nonsense or conceit about them at all. The country they thrived in was just too brutal for anything but survival. Everything had to be of value to the Apache or else they either ate it or shot it and left it behind.

Take horses for example. A Kiowa or a Comanche prized his horse more than his squaw. But an Apache would take a good, strong horse and ride it to the point of death. And then, he would climb off the poor thing and cut its throat and eat its meat raw.

Apache were the toughest, deadliest, and most dangerous men alive to Clint's way of thinking, and he had seen a lifetime of hard, heartless men. You showed no mercy to the Apache because they did not know the meaning of the word except to their own kind.

And if . . . God forbid, if Miss Judy had already fallen into their hands, he hoped she had known enough to kill herself at the very first opportunity.

For a white woman, death was better than being the slave of the Apache. Anyone who did not know that much did not know the Apache at all.

# THIRTEEN

Miss Judy Monroe was desperate and yet she had maintained her composure every step of the way from Union City to the Arizona border. She had been warned by the Gunsmith that the men she had chosen to guide her into the Apache stronghold were inept, bungling, and unfamiliar with the country they were to invade. She had believed the Gunsmith and gone ahead anyway, hoping beyond reason that he might change his mind out of concern for her and catch up.

But Clint Adams had not pursued her. And after days of glancing around on their back-trail, the realization that she was on her own with these two men hit her like a brick in the face. She had almost panicked and turned her horse around, but something inside of her that she supposed was pure mule-headedness or stiff-backed southern pride forbid her to do so. Instead, she had just continued on mile after grueling mile. They had gotten lost coming off the Sangre de Cristos and had traveled too far north before turning south. They had ridden miles out of their way and, as a consequence, had ended up climbing through the rugged Mogollon Mountains in west-central New Mexico. For three days, they had scrambled up and down treacherous slopes and game trails. They had almost drowned in a thundering river whose name she did not know and never wanted to see again.

Finally, Judy had called a halt to things and forced a showdown. She had told the men that they were useless, worse than useless. They were dangerous because they pretended to know things that they did not.

Shorty and Vince had argued in their own self-defense and, when that failed, they had become surly and uncooperative.

Judy fired them. They refused to leave her and insisted they had a stake in the Lost Apache Mine. And that was how things stood right up until this very minute. The two had dropped all pretense of knowing where they were heading. They had ended up using the North star as their guide and they followed the rivers, which always seemed to run south. But they were really lost. They might be riding straight down into Mexico for all any of them knew.

Judy was scared. And hot. The temperature in the desert was well over a hundred in the afternoon, and they were forced to hole up wherever they could find a spot of shade or water.

"Hey, look!" Shorty cried from under the shade of a pinion tree. "I see something moving out there!"

Judy was on her feet instantly. "Get the horses out of sight!" she cried, seeing a distant figure on the horizon and fearing it might be an Apache scout.

"You get the damned horses," Vince snapped. "I ain't leaving this shade."

"Me, neither," Shorty said. "We ain't afraid of one man on foot."

"Then I'll do it myself."

Judy wanted to shoot those two for their laziness and insubordination. She was paying for their food and supplies. Paying for everything. That should have meant that they obeyed her orders. Since Vince and Shorty had ran out of whiskey, their personalities had changed dramatically. All the bravado they had exhibited in Union City had evaporated the moment they had been out of sight of that town. Now, they were surly and ill-tempered nearly all the time. They constantly complained and refused to follow her orders.

Judy did not know what to do with them. Her only consolation was that, if the Apaches did strike, at least she would have two guns beside her because, even though shiftless, Vince and Shorty would also be fighting for their very lives.

She moved all three of their horses back into the rocks and drew her own rifle out of the saddle boot. Her dear father had taught her how to shoot, and she had no reservations about doing so if it meant preserving her life.

"It ain't no damned Indian," Vince said, standing up and shading his eyes against the harsh sunlight. "And that's a burro, not a horse he's leading."

"It's probably just some old prospector lookin' for a handout," Shorty said, hitching up his pants and blowing his nose lustily.

Judy relaxed as the figure came nearer. She could see now that it was an old man who posed no threat. "I believe you're right," she said to Shorty. "He is a prospector."

They could see a pick and a big gold pan strapped to the side of the little burro. When the man reached them, he squinted from watery eyes buried in a brown, wrinkled face. "What the hell are you three dudes doin' down in this Apache country?" he snorted.

Judy was momentarily taken aback by his rudeness.

"We are. . . ." She wasn't sure whether or not she should tell the prospector they were searching for gold.

"We got a map to the Lost Apache Mine!" Shorty said, swaggering up to the prospector and grinning with an air of superiority. "We're going to find us a mountain of gold and come back rich."

The prospector hawked and spat a stream of tobacco juice that splattered across Shorty's dusty boots. "All you're going to get, pilgrims, is your scalps and some other private parts lifted. There ain't no Lost Apache Mine, fer chrissakes! I been prospecting this country on and off for twenty years now. Don't you think I'd know if there was such a thing!"

Judy did not see any point in arguing with the cantankerous old man. "We have a little food," she said, "and some water and shade. Would you like to share it with us until it cools off?"

The prospector looked at them carefully. His deepset eyes took their measure and he said, "I guess you three are about as harmless as they come. Sure, I'll sit a spell and rest my burro. Then I got to get moving along. This country ain't safe right now. Ain't safe at all!"

Judy exchanged glances with Shorty and Vince. Their belligerence was replaced by worry. "What do you mean by that?" she asked. "It was my understanding that the Chiricuahas are *always* dangerous."

"You're going up into the Chiricuahas!"

"Yes. That's where the mine is to be found."

The prospector shook his head sadly and wiped the sweat from his brow with the back of his wrist. He was average-sized, yet had the shoulders and arms of a young man. His hands were grossly outsized, and Judy guessed it was because of all the years of swinging a pick and lifting tons of worthless rock. "Ma'am," he said, "I sure wish you'd change yer mind about going on ahead. You see, you was dead right when you said them mountains was dangerous. But sometimes, the Apache are down raiding in Mexico, and a man can sneak in there and do a little prospecting."

"And I take it this isn't one of those times," Judy said.

"You couldn't have picked a worse time, ma'am. You see, them Apache are tough as rawhide but they don't like the desert heat any more than white folks like us. So they usually come north out of Mexico and summer in the Chiricahuas. And then, there are the Mexican banditos."

Shorty exclaimed, "You mean we got a bunch of damned greasers to worry about, too!"

The prospector nodded. "They're in cahoots with the Apache, and some of them are worse than the Apache themselves. They buy slaves from the Indians and sell them back to their families down in Mexico. Zamora is the Apache chief who does most of the kidnapping of Mexican women and children. He just caves in the heads of the growed ups."

Judy shuddered. "Zamora. Where does he summer?"

The prospector pointed even farther northwest. Fifty miles away they could see the faint outline of mountains. "Those are the bloody Chiricahuas. The U.S. Army has never been able to chase the Apache out of 'em, and I doubt they ever will. Zamora is chief of the Chiricahua Apache, and he don't ever camp the same place so they can get a line on him. He moves all the time. If you are up there and he's in the same mountains, he'll find you."

"Maybe we ought to wait until fall when he goes south," Vince said nervously.

"That'd be a good idea," the prospector said. "But there's always some Apache up there and there ain't no safe time. Just some worse than others."

"I'm going on now," Judy said. "I'm not waiting until fall or winter to get caught in the snow."

The prospector shrugged. "You suit yourself. They'll torture and scalp them two buzzards you're hangin' out with. But you ma'am, you'll be kept alive as a slave. You're so durn pretty that Zamora might even take you for a wife hisself. He's got a weakness for white women. Likes 'em better than Apache or Mex, even. But he likes 'em little fatter'n you."

Judy shuddered. She cleared her throat and managed to say, "I thank you for the warning, but it doesn't change anything. We're going on."

"Being pretty don't necessarily mean you got good brains," the old prospector said.

Judy said nothing. She sat down on a hot rock and studied the distant blue mountains with a mixture of fear and fierce determination. She would not turn back!

# FOURTEEN

They reached the base of the Chiricahuas at daybreak and then began the long climb up their eastern slopes. Judy was as worried about the lack of water as she was the Apache. They carried canteens but you could not water a horse for long on that little amount. The slopes they scaled were littered with cactus and the brassy sun hammered the rocks so that the heatwaves undulated along the contours of the mountainside.

Their horses scrambled and fought to climb higher to a cooler land, but it was clear they were suffering from heat prostration. And because there was no place to find shelter until they reached the pines several thousand feet above them, they pushed on.

Shorty's horse quit at noon. It had stopped sweating, and they all knew that the horse would die without water. They gave it a hatful but the animal was already shaking so bad it could not drink. Finally, it dropped and began to thrash.

"Please put your animal out of its misery," Judy said quietly. "Even if we had water, it would be too late now."

Shorty drew his revolver.

"Not your gun!" Vince shouted. "Use your knife and cut its throat."

Judy turned away from the sight. Of course they could not afford to fire a bullet and have the sound carry across the miles of mountainside. She sleeved angry tears and climbed off her Thoroughbred, for she would lead it up the rest of the way to the top. The horse was huffing badly but was still able to sweat.

"Hey!" Shorty cried a few minutes later as he wiped the blade of his knife on his pantsleg, "what am I supposed to do, walk all over these mountains!"

Judy stopped. Turned. "Maybe we can steal a horse from the Indians," she said. "Until then, you and Vince can ride double when we get on flat ground."

"The hell with that! You got the biggest horse. I'll ride double with you on that Thoroughbred."

"No," she said. Judy knew full well that, if they ran into Indian trouble, Shorty would shove her off the Thoroughbred and make a run for it leaving both her and Vince to face the Apache. "You stay clear away from my horse."

"My God! I'm not going to take any more orders from you, woman!"

He started for her, and Vince did not move a muscle to help her. Judy yanked her rifle out of its boot and levered in a shell. "Throw your gun down and move away from it," she said, "or so help me, I'll blow your head off."

Shorty started to ignore her warning and make a rush but she was uphill of him and he knew that there was no chance of overpowering her before she could fire a bullet.

"This ain't right," Shorty hissed. "Vince, you know this ain't right. In this country, a man afoot is a dead man. Ain't he? Ain't he, Vince!"

"Why don't you turn around and go on back," Vince said coldly. "We'll give you some water, and you can probably make it if you sip and travel only by day."

Shorty screamed, "And *you* will probably waltz with me into hell! No, sir, I'm not facing that fifty miles of desert again on foot. No, sir!"

He was staring out at the desert they had just crossed, and Judy didn't blame him for refusing to attempt to return on foot. Even on horseback, the desert had been like an inferno and every mile of the way had been a torture. Judy knew in her heart that Shorty would die out there someplace.

"We'll be over the top and in the pines by late afternoon," she said. "We'll find water and grass for the horses."

"How far is the mine from here?"

"I don't know exactly," she said, stalling the question.

"Dammit but I wished you hadn't burned your uncle's map!"

"I told you that I had memorized it first," she said. "It's in my mind for safekeeping."

Judy no longer felt the same guilt she had felt when she had first sewn her uncle's map into the lining of her skirts and then told the pair she had burned it. After riding the trail with these men for over a week, it was clear that she had done the right thing. If they could have gotten their hands on the map and left her to die in the desert, they would have done so in a minute. The only thing that was keeping them beside her was the promise of a golden fortune.

"Come on," she said wearily. "The slope won't get any flatter by standing on it."

Shorty anguished over leaving his saddle behind, but he did not think enough of it to cut the latigo and hoist it over his shoulder. All he bothered to cut loose from the dead horse was his canteen, rifle, bedroll, and a sack of dried apricots he had insisted on her buying for him along the way.

It was nearly dark when they reached the top of the mountain. They were all staggering with exhaustion, and the horses were withering fast. But only a mile before them, almost as if her prayers had finally been answered, was a small grassy meadow fed by a clear mountain stream.

"We're saved," Vince gasped as he climbed onto his horse and whipped it into a stumbling run toward the mountains. "We're saved!"

Judy mounted up, too.

"Don't leave me!" Shorty cried. "Wait for me!"

Judy waited. She resisted his attempt to grab her horse and pull himself up behind her saddle. She made him walk, and he cursed her vilely but that only lasted until they reached the stream and then everything was all right.

That night, she was so weary she fell asleep without eating any supper. She slept until the sound of a hammer cocking back woke her. The sun was high above the meadow and the pines, but all she saw was Shorty with his gun pointed at her breast.

"Draw us the map," he hissed. "Draw it up right now in the dirt so's we can memorize it, or so help me, I'll blow a hole in you with your own damn gun!"

"Then go ahead and kill me, because I won't be left behind to die up here!"

The gun shook in Shorty's small fist. But he did not shoot because she alone knew the whereabouts of the mine. Shorty looked to Vince and raised his bushy eyebrows in question.

"All right," Vince spat with the gall of defeat bitter in his throat. "You win. But before we go any farther, we want to know where the mine is. If something should accidentally happen to you, we'd be stuck with nothing for taking all this risk and trouble. It's only fair."

Judy supposed that, had she been dealing with men she trusted, their logic did make sense and their demand was fair. But she did not trust these men, and she was not about to tell them everything. Just enough to get them close. It seemed clear to her that this was the only intelligent thing to do.

"Well," Shorty demanded with impatience, "what's it going to be!"

Lucy studied the man's ravaged face. He seemed to have aged a great deal since Union City and so had his partner, Vince. They were both a couple of worthless scoundrels and deserved to be caught by the Apache for this treachery.

"Draw the map!" Vince said. "Or I'll use my knife to carve you up like a holiday turkey!"

"All right," she whispered with anger boiling under the surface where they could not see it. "But I should have listened to Clint Adams when he said you two were not to be trusted."

"Lady," Shorty said, "he didn't seem like no choirboy hisself to me."

Vince gave her a pointed stick. She rolled over and smoothed a broad patch of dirt and hesitated only a moment before she began to draw.

"This," she began, "is Red-Toothed Mountain. We'll know it because it's the only red-colored one in all of the Chiricahuas. It is still north of here, I'm sure of that much."

"How do you know?" Vince demanded.

"Because this stream is called Sparkling Sun by the Apache, and if we follow it we should eventually come to a pair of twin lakes called The Two Moons."

She drew the stream to the lakes and then added Red-Toothed Mountain.

"I thought you said you was lost," Shorty said angrily. "Hell, you knew all the time we'd find water up here and be all right!"

"No, I didn't. This mountain range stretches over a hundred miles north and south. It could be ten miles or fifty to The Two Moons. I don't have any idea. I'd guess we'd see Red-Toothed Mountain long before we'll see those lakes."

"So where is this Lost Apache Mine?" Vince asked, leaning forward, his face reflecting both his greed and eagerness.

"After we pass the lakes and that mountain, we veer east and travel ten miles to a sheer rock cliff that faces directly south. We go around that cliff and climb a small hill until we come to a valley."

"A valley. Christ!" Shorty stormed. "This whole mountain range is full of valleys."

"This one will have a bunch of lightning-blasted trees at its entrance. We go up the valley to its very end."

Vince licked his lips and fidgeted nervously. "And then what?"

Judy threw the stick away. "And then I'll draw you one more map that will carry us the last ten miles to the Lost Apache Mine."

Shorty grabbed her by the hair and wrenched her head back. He yanked out his big hunting knife and pressed it to her throat. Judy felt the cold steel and she tensed, expecting the man might actually lose his senses and kill her on the spot.

"You'll tell us right now!" he raged.

"No," she managed to choke.

He threw her down on her blankets and roared with

anger and frustration. "Damn you, woman! Ten miles ain't good enough!"

There were tears in her eyes and her heart was beating so fast that she thought sure that it was going to burst. But there was cold fury, too. Her father had killed in anger, though that was long before he had become a judge and a gentleman. He had confessed to her he had also lost his head during the Civil War and killed Union soldiers. It was not a thing he either took pride or pain in recalling. In war, honor meant very little and winning nearly everything.

But now, for the very first time in her life, Judy understood real hatred. She had stood beside the Gunsmith and her father to face the Corbetts, but she had done so out of a sense of duty and honor. A code driven into her almost from birth by her father. But this . . . this murderous feeling she had inside for these two vile creatures had nothing to do with honor.

"It will have to be good enough until we get there!" she cried. "I will be damned if I will tell you where the gold is to be found."

Vince swore loud and long. "She means it, Shorty. She ain't bluffin'."

He put away his knife. "Well, neither am I," he spat. "And she better tell us the rest when we get there or I'll finish her off just like I did the horse."

"I'll tell you," Judy said. "Now let me up and let's ride out of here."

The two men let her up and ten minutes later, Shorty and Vince were doubled up on one horse and she was leading them north along the streambed. They had not given her back her weapons. That meant that she was their hostage and if they were jumped by Indians, she was going to have to use her Thoroughbred's speed to leave them behind.

# FIFTEEN

Clint reached the Chiricahuas at sunset. He rested his horse until midnight and then he reined Duke into the high mountains. The desert air had cooled and the big gelding's work was made much easier as it climbed steadily through the long night. By daybreak man and horse were into the sweet-scented pines and picking a cautious trail north.

Hadn't there been a stream to follow? He was not sure, but he did need to find water within the next day. A horse needed gallons of the stuff just to survive in this rugged country.

The Gunsmith wished that he had studied the map of the Lost Apache Mine a little more closely. He remembered Red-Toothed Mountain because Miss Judy's uncle had underlined it in red, and the young lady had explained that it was at the northern end of this mountain range, the only one of its kind.

After that, Clint remembered very little. He knew that he could not find the mine himself and that was the way he wanted it. The Lost Apache, if there really was such a mine, belonged to either the Apache or to Miss Judy. It did not belong to him, and he wanted no part of it.

Actually, for one of the very first times in his life, he had a great deal of money, thanks to poor Lotta Cooper, who had named him the beneficiary of her estate. Lotta had bequeathed the Gunsmith every cent she owned, and it came to more than five thousand dollars. Clint did not need that kind of money, and he guessed he'd give most of it away to some of his poorest friends, male and female.

It was the Gunsmith's observation that a man who kept a lot of idle money in the bank wound up worrying all the time about how that money could make more money. You would think if a fella had a lot of extra money, he'd give no thought to it, but the exact opposite was true. The greater the wealth a man had, the harder he worked to accumulate even more. Clint had a theory that too little money made men mean, but too much made them small-minded and grasping. He sorta figured it best to have a couple of hundred dollars stashed away here and there and let it go at that.

In the two days that followed his entry into the Chiricahuas, the Gunsmith rode with his pistol loose in its holster and every sense keyed to danger. He crossed many trails and campfires and they all looked fresh. He saw the signs of unshod Apache horses everywhere, and it made the hairs on the back of his neck stand up and quiver.

And then on the third morning, he ran into the Apache and his blood turned cold. There were just two and normally, they would have been almost impossible to see first. However, Clint had the rare good fortune of coming upon them just after they had discovered Miss Judy's trail.

The Apache were very excited. They were talking loud, making wild gestures and running back and forth across the tracks. They would point one direction and then another. It

seemed to the Gunsmith that there was some strong dis-
agreement between them as to whether they should follow
the trail of the three whites or maybe alert their own camp
first and get additional warriors to pursue the invaders.

Clint dismounted in the trees. He watched the argument
rage for nearly an hour knowing that, if the pair of Apache
scouts angled off the trail to alert their tribe, he was going
to have to stop them in a big hurry. But if they decided to
follow Miss Judy and overtake her by themselves, he
would let them lead him, for he could have no better
trackers.

The Apache decided to return to their camp.

"Damn!" Clint whispered bitterly. She led Duke out of
the pine into plain view. He *had* to kill the Apache or else
Miss Judy and her two companions were already as good
as dead.

"Come on and fight!" he yelled, breaking the mountain
silence.

The Apache had been about to mount their starving
ponies when Clint's challenge split the mountain silence.
The two Indians spun in unison and their knives were in
their hands and held out before their muscular bodies as if
they had practiced that deadly move in their sleep.

Clint spied a broken limb about four feet long and as thick
as his forearm. The wood was aged white by the sun and the
bark was eroded away. He picked it up and was satisfied by
its solid heft. The easiest and by far the safest thing to do at
this point would be to just shoot the Apache when they came
charging in at him. But the retort of his sixgun would bounce
and echo for miles in these mountains and canyons, and he
wanted to avoid that if at all possible.

So as the Apache swung onto their ponies and came
flying across the mile of rocky ground that separated them,
Clint tore a few of the small branches off his long, jagged
stick and then mounted Duke. He was going to have to kill

this pair, and he was going to try to do it with this damned spear.

The Gunsmith shook his head and longed to pull his sixgun and abruptly end this affair neat and clean. The spear-shaped limb in his hand felt awkward and he knew that he was outmatched in this sort of combat. Duke trembled and danced and it was easy to see why. The Apache were screaming their heads off and they looked scary and mean enough to whip their weight in wildcats. Dammit, Clint thought, feeling sweat break out across his torso, why was it that nothing came easy in this life?

When the two Apache were still fifty yards away, Clint put his reins between his teeth and gripped the branch with both hands. He said a little prayer and touched Duke with his spurs and the gelding leapt forward like an armored knight's medieval charger in a jousting match. Clint waited until they were closing and then he swung Duke hard to the left so that he was not forced to race between them as they had planned. He reared back with the branch and swung with all his strength as he came abreast of the Apache. The heavy branch struck the Indian in the throat and knocked him spinning.

The second Apache screamed in anger. He wheeled his pony and charged again. Clint reined Duke around and hoped that he could repeat his earlier success. But the second Apache cheated. The man did not wait until they came together but instead, he hurled his spear, and Clint had no choice but to throw himself completely out of the saddle or he would have been skewered through the belly.

He struck the dirt hard and rolled. The Apache yelled in triumph and came racing back for the kill. He tried to drive his horse into the woozy Gunsmith, but Clint whacked the Indian pony across the muzzle so hard the tree limb broke in two pieces. The animal reared, tossing the Apache to the ground. The Indian bounced up and charged with his knife.

Clint jabbed him in the chest with the jagged end of his broken tree limb and, though it stopped the Apache warrior, it did not seriously injure him.

The Apache dove for Clint and his knife sliced for Clint's underbelly. The blade scraped hard against his belt buckle and slashed down through the holster and his six-gun.

Clint backed up knowing he should have been disemboweled. "Come and get it," he said, trying to rouse his own flagging spirits. "Or better yet, why don't we shake hands and pretend we are friends? You go your way, I'll go mine. Peace, huh?"

The Indian snarled and slashed again. He did not seem at all interested in palavering about friendship.

Clint slashed at him with the broken limb and the Apache ducked. During that split-second that Clint was off balance, the Apache lunged in for the kill. Clint saw it, knew he was completely exposed, and that a death blow was coming his way. He did the only thing he could do to save his life—as he fell, the Gunsmith drew his gun and put a bullet through the Apache's brain.

Clint listened to the retort of his sixgun echo through the silent mountains, and he cursed because he had been forced to use his gun. He stood up and walked over to the first Apache that he had unhorsed. The blow had broken the warrior's neck.

The Gunsmith picked up his broken limb and hurled it as far as he could. He had not wanted to kill this pair and he had especially not wanted to do it with a gun.

There had been no choice. The second Apache had beaten him cold. Clint walked over to the Indian ponies. If he let them go, they would eventually drift back to the Apache village where they belonged. He could not allow that to happen. Clint tied the ponies together and then roped them to his saddlehorn. Two extra horses might come in handy, even a pair as thin and pitiful as these.

Clint had one more job to do and that was to drag the dead Apache into the rocks and cover them from sight and from animals. It took him almost an hour and it was not a pleasant task. Before he mounted Duke, he used the bough of a pine tree to sweep away all signs of his passing and of the skirmish.

Duke was shod, and there was nothing he could do about that if the Apache crossed his trail. True, he would have two unshod Indian ponies coming along behind to partly obliterate Duke's hoofprints, but partly wasn't near good enough.

Sooner or later—probably sooner—the Apache would come looking for the two dead warriors, and they would pick up the trail of the Gunsmith, Miss Judy, and her two worthless companions.

Clint sat very quietly in his saddle. He remembered how his lone gunshot had echoed on forever. Maybe, he thought, the Apache are coming already.

# SIXTEEN

Judy knew they were in trouble the moment she opened her eyes and saw her horse raise its head and whinny. Dawn was just peeking over the eastern horizon and the air was crisp. Their campfire was smoking and that was what must have led the danger to them.

"Wake up!" she whispered, reaching for her gun and rolling from under her blankets. "Wake up!"

Shorty and Vince were on their feet in an instant. "What the hell is wrong!" Shorty cried, staring wildly and turning a full circle.

"Look at our horses," Judy said. "There are other horses out there. Someone is coming."

"Oh, Jesus," Vince moaned. "It's gotta be Apache! Let's get the hell out of here!"

"No!" Judy said. "We've got a better chance here in these rocks than out there in the open. Where could we possibly run? It's a hundred miles to a town or a military fort. This is all we've got!"

The two men were nearly in a panic, but her logic was so sound that it managed to penetrate their fevered minds. They ducked down into the rocks and stared into the dawn.

"We have to bring the horses in closer," Vince said. "If they get the horses, we can kiss our asses so long."

Judy nodded. She grabbed her rifle and said, "I'll cover you both. Bring them right into these rocks and tie them to the pine tree over there. We only run as a last resort. Agreed?"

The two nodded. Even in the half-light, she could see that their faces were pasty with fear.

"Go on!" she urged.

They went over the rocks and raced for the horses. Judy held her breath and watched as they unhobbled the two animals and began to lead them at a trot back into the rocks. So far, so good. Just having her Thoroughbred close gave her a measure of strength that had been missing moments ago.

But even as she watched, a volley of riflefire exploded from a stand of timber. Judy slapped the stock of her rifle to her shoulder and fired three rounds back knowing that she would hit nothing but wanting to do something.

Shorty dropped the rope to her Thoroughbred and raced for the safety of camp. Vince yelled, "Come back here, you stupid bastard!"

But Shorty kept running. The Thoroughbred almost broke free and ran. With her heart in her throat, Judy hopped over the rocks and raced out into the swarm of bullets to help control the high-spirited animal.

Despite the fact that bullets were flying all around them, they somehow managed to get the two frightened animals into the rocks.

"Goddam you!" Vince yelled at his partner. "Without the Thoroughbred, none of us got a chance of getting outta these mountains alive!"

It was true and extremely obvious, but when Vince put into words the very thought that had comforted her, Judy felt a tremor of real fear. All three of them were planning on using the racehorse if things got bad, and from the looks of it right now, things were getting bad fast.

A body of mounted horsemen materialized from the trees. The sunrise was blinding, but Judy could tell in an instant that the men who had fired upon them were not Indians, because silver glinted off their outfits and they wore the wide-brimmed sombreros.

"Mexican banditos!" Vince hissed.

Judy expelled an involuntary sigh of relief because anything was preferable to Apache.

"Look!" Shorty cried. "The one on the white horse wants to talk."

"I'm going to shoot the bastard," Vince spat, raising his Winchester to peer down the sights.

"No!" Judy knocked the barrel of the gun down, and it exploded into the rocks, sending splinters into their legs.

"Damn you!" Vince shouted. "Why'd you do that!"

"Because maybe we can strike a deal," she said. "We *have* to strike a deal if we want to get out of this mess alive."

"I ain't talking to him," Shorty vowed.

Judy stood up. "Then I will."

They did not try to stop her, though she almost wished they would. She had never been so afraid of dying in her entire life. And as she walked out to meet the leader of the bandits, she could see that the man was smiling and his eyes were raping her with every stride she took.

What can I give him in trade for our freedom, she thought desperately. If I gave him my body he would give me nothing in return and use me like a whore. I would rather be dead. If I told about the Lost Apache Mine, he might be stalled into saving us in hopes of getting everything when we reached the mine. What good would that do? It would make him rich and us dead in a few more days. But I *must* tell him something. I must have some reason for being here that he will believe.

Try as she might, she could think of nothing.

"Señorita," he said, flashing a set of the whitest teeth she had ever seen. "My name is José Luis Ortega Escobar and you are beautiful! What brings one such as you to such a country as this?"

Judy stopped only a few feet from his white stallion. "I am searching for . . . gold," she stammered. "I have heard there is a rich gold mine in these mountains."

The Mexican threw his head back and laughed. It was not a nice laugh. He was short and fat with black eyes, black hair, and pounds of silver jewelry on his wrists and his fingers. A brilliantly colored serape was thrown over his right shoulder and a bandolier of bullets was slung over the other shoulder. Two pearl-handled pistols were jammed into his waistband, and a big knife protruded from his hand-stitched boottops. Clearly, this was a vain man and Judy tried to think of a way to exploit that weakness to her advantage. The man had at least thirty banditos and though they had remained a distance away, they looked very deadly.

"I very sure that there is no gold hidden in these mountains. But you are a very good-looking woman, senorita!"

"Thank you. You . . . you, Señor Escobar, are a handsome and flattering man."

"Perhaps we should become better acquainted," he said, leaning forward across his oversized saddlehorn. "Would you like that?"

"Perhaps," she said, trying to smile and knowing she was not close to succeeding. She turned to compose her expression again. "Those are my friends. Shorty and Vince."

"I will talk to them later," Escobar said, dismounting and motioning for one of his men to ride forward and take the reins of his horse.

He came forward, and she could smell him he reeked so strongly. He stopped before her and bowed, then straightened with a smile. "You look even better up close, señorita."

She took a backstep, but he reached out and grabbed her wrist saying, "Come with me for a walk into the forest."

"No!" She tried to resist and not to panic, but he was not a gentleman and ignored her plea. Judy was suddenly filled with terror. She had never met anyone like this. Everything was out of control and moving so terribly fast.

She dug her heels into the dirt, and the other Mexican banditos began to hoot and laugh. Their behavior inflamed her southern pride, and she jumped forward and clawed Escobar's round face. Her fingernails tore strips of skin away, and he yelped in pain and fury.

For a moment, she was free and turned to run. He was coming after her. They all were. Judy glanced over her shoulder and saw that Escobar was too fat to overtake her on foot. She would make it if. . . .

The banditos opened fire at her, and then Shorty and Vince began to shoot back at them. Everything was chaos. Judy heard a high-pitched scream and glanced back to see that Escobar had been shot in the thigh and was down.

Breath tearing in and out of her lungs, she flew into the rocks and grabbed her rifle.

"So much for talk," she gasped, "we're fighting for our lives now."

She opened fire and a bandito died in his saddle.

# SEVENTEEN

Judy Monroe looked up and saw that the sunset had cast a crimson curtain across the southern Arizona skies. It was a beautiful sunset and she supposed that it might very well be the last she would ever see. They had held off José Luis Ortega Escobar and his banditos all day long, but now their ammunition was almost gone, and the Mexicans were moving in for the kill.

"We've finished," Shorty said, his voice high and quavery. "We might as well try to strike some kind of a deal. Any kind of a deal!"

But Judy shook his head. "There is no deal to be made. Besides, when one of you shot Escobar, we sealed our fates. Haven't you heard the man screaming curses all afternoon?"

"We don't know any Spanish," Vince said.

"You don't need to understand the language, all you have to do is to listen to the hatred in his voice."

It was true. The Mexican bandit's pride had been deeply

wounded. First, because Judy had spurned him in front of his men, and second because she had managed to escape and make him look foolish in a losing footrace. Judy did not claim to know men, but she recognized unbridled vanity when she saw it, and Escobar, with all his fancy silver and embroidered clothes, was a very vain man.

"Well, what are we going to do, then?" Shorty asked. "If we stay here in the dark, those greasers will come flying over the rocks in the dark and use their filthy pigstickers to cut our throats."

"Shorty is right," Vince said. "We're almost out of bullets. Those sonsabitches can see better in the dark than we can. We stay here, we ain't got a chance of making it alive until morning."

"We don't have any choice but to stay," Judy argued. "Maybe . . . maybe we can. . . ."

"The hell with all this talk!" Shorty yelled. "I'm sick and tired of taking orders from a damned woman. I say we get out while the getting is good."

Judy turned around to try to talk him into some sense. Maybe they could escape, but not until the banditos had relaxed their guard. Right now, they were expecting such a move. The Mexicans would be waiting to gun them down the moment they tried to break out and run.

She took a deep breath. "If you'll only—"

Judy never finished her sentence. Shorty's fist crashed into her jaw, and a cry of pain died on her lips as she fell, striking her head against a rock. She had never been punched in the face before and was amazed to discover that, while the blow delivered by Shorty in conjunction with striking the rock had not knocked her unconscious, it stunned her so that she had no control over her body. She couldn't move.

Shorty yanked her rifle away and said, "Let's get our

horses and ride the hell outta these damned mountains now!"

Vince hesitated. "You just want to leave her? What about that lost gold mine?"

"You can't spend it if you're dead. My only regret is that we put off using her for our pleasure, and now it's too late."

"The greasers will do that for us and if they leave anything, so will the Apache. It'd be merciful to shoot her right now."

"Don't waste a bullet," Shorty hissed. "Let's ride!"

"I get her Thoroughbred."

"The hell you do!"

"I weigh more than you do by thirty pounds."

"Yeah," Shorty yelled, "so because you're too fat, does that mean I'm supposed to ride a slow horse!"

"Damn right!" Vince stormed.

Judy heard them arguing violently. She tried to raise her head but could not. Then, a single shot rang out and she heard a groan as Vince cried, "Shorty, you can't leave me here to die."

"Watch me," he said.

A moment later, the sound of a horse could be heard galloping hard over the rocky shelf they were camped upon.

A volley of riflefire exploded across her consciousness and after the echoes, the Chiricahuas were very silent.

It was only minutes later that she heard the sounds of spur rowels raking the rock. A gunshot exploded almost in her ear, and Judy knew that Vince was dead and so was Shorty. It made her want to cry. They had betrayed and abandoned her, but at least they were familiar and might have been reasoned with. But Judy knew that she was doomed to an unspeakable fate at the hands of the Mexican banditos.

Rough hands pulled her erect, and she was thrown over a man's shoulder. He smelled of grease, chili, and smoke. A Mexican said something and then he patted her on the behind and was able to slip his hand up and down her dress to her knees. There was laughter, and she was carried downhill into the Mexican camp.

Judy was terrified. She felt a tingling in her hands and feet, and now she was able to wiggle her toes. A few moments later, she knew that the effect of Shorty's blow had completely disappeared.

She squeezed her eyes shut very tightly. She was roughly tossed on a blanket, and she pretended to be unconscious as the talk swirled around her.

"Wake up!" She recognized the leader's guttural voice and refused to open her eyes.

Suddenly, Escobar's dirty hand grabbed her lower jaw and wrenched it downward. Judy tried to lock her teeth but the leader of the banditos above her pinched into her cheeks with the sharp nails of his thumb and forefinger. The pain was so excruciating that she cried out, and when she did, a bottle of vile liquor was shoved between her teeth. The fiery liquid was poured down her throat.

Coughing and choking, she sat up amid the laughter of the bandits. Her long hair hung over her face as she tried to spit out the Mexican poison.

"It is the honey of the cactus!" Escobar proclaimed. "It is tequila. You want some more, my little flower?"

She shook her head violently. Escobar took a fistful of her hair and threw her back down on the blanket. His foul breath filled her nostrils, and his tongue tried to enter her mouth. He ripped at her clothes. Judy fought him like a wildcat, but he was so strong and heavy it was no use. The other banditos were shouting and jumping up and down with delight and anticipation.

Judy gasped as Escobar's fingers probed her woman-hood, and then suddenly, his corpulent body froze over her.

"*Madre mia!*" he rumbled in a tone of disbelief. "You are a . . . a virgin?"

She could neither speak nor lift her eyes to their faces. All she could do was nod her head.

This admission caused a stir among the bandits, and a storm of conversation that abruptly terminated when Escobar yanked out his pistol and fired it into the sky.

"Untorn, your flower is worth a small fortune to Zamora," Escobar said. "He is angry with me, but my gift of you will soothe that eagle's feathers."

Judy remembered. Zamora was the chief of the Chiricahua Apache. Zamora was the one that the old prospector had warned her about.

"Please," she whispered, "let me go."

"Do you think I am *loco!*" Escobar shouted. He barked a short laugh. "I am not *loco!* You will win me Zamora's friendship, and these mountains will become my sanctuary from those who would kill me."

Escobar gave orders to his men. Judy was pulled erect, and now for the first time, she looked at the Mexican leader. He had a bloody bandage wrapped around his big thigh, but it was obvious it was only a flesh wound. He glared at her and said, "You would have been happier if you had gone with me into the forest when you had the chance. Now you will become an Apache slave. You will learn the meaning of hell."

Despite all her resolve, the tears streamed down her face, and that made the bandits laugh very loud.

# EIGHTEEN

Clint Adams saw the vultures before he reached the high, rocky plateau, and those huge black birds made his blood run cold. I am too late, he thought. Miss Judy is dead.

He yanked his well-used and well-oiled Winchester rifle out of its saddle scabbard and levered in a shell. Some of the vultures were on the ground, and that would normally mean that there were no live humans around to frighten them away. But more than one white man had died making that false assumption. The Apache were so stealthy that they even fooled buzzards. It would be just like the Apache to wait if they suspected a white man was coming along their trail.

The Gunsmith rode light in the saddle. As he approached, the buzzards beat their great wings up and down and hopped threateningly. They made terrible squawking noises, but Clint ignored them and his eyes never stopped moving over the rocks, the trees, and the cover surrounding this place of death.

He did not want to see Miss Judy if the Indians had used and then killed her. But he had to find out. The moment he rode into their camp, Clint knew she wasn't dead. The Gunsmith had never pretended to be the world's best tracker, but during his years as a lawman he had developed all the rudimentary skills and put them into everyday practice. He was still able to read a story out of what he found on the trail or around an old campfire.

This story behind this camp and the battle that had resulted in Shorty's and Vincent's deaths was not difficult to decipher. The wind had not scattered the embers of their campfire and spur-roweled tracks of the Mexican banditos remained very clear.

When he had learned all that was important from the camp, Clint followed the track of Judy's fine Thoroughbred for almost an hour before it was joined by the unshod tracks of Apache ponies. Clint turned around and rode back to the camp, knowing that some Indian was going to ride a very fast horse until the beast grew weak and was butchered.

The Gunsmith took up the trail of the Mexican banditos. And even though he guessed there were between twelve and fifteen, he was not as cautious as he might have been had the captors been Apache. The banditos would not be expecting a lone man to be following them. And not surprisingly, the trail they traveled veered away from Red-Toothed Mountain. That meant that Judy had not told the banditos why she was in the Chiricahuas.

"If it's there," he said to his horse, "it could be our ace-in-the-hole. Our only real chance to work a deal to get out of these damned mountains alive."

Duke bobbed his head as if to say that nothing would

please him more. He acted very uneasy in a land inhabited by Indians who preferred horse meat to beef.

Because he had ridden hard in order to overtake Miss Judy, he was forced to release the two Indian ponies, who could not keep up with Duke. Clint did this with some reluctance because they might have come in very handy when he tried to rescue Miss Judy. In the days that followed, the Gunsmith rode over one mountain after another. The trails were faint and often dangerous with tall cliffs and the kind of loose gravel that got a man on a horse in deep trouble. He heard mountain lions scream at night and though it was farther south than the normal range of grizzly bears, he saw vicious claw marks high up on the trunks of pine trees that told him grizzlies were very much a part of this wild northern Chiricahua Mountain range. Surprisingly, he found plenty of water, but then he was at the northern end of the mountain range and the southern part was drier and trailed all the way down into Mexico.

Clint was within hours of the Mexicans, and thinking about how he might free Miss Judy was the main thought on his mind. When he came to a ridge, something told him that he had better dismount and approach it on foot. The Gunsmith tied his horse to a manzanita bush and hiked up near the top of the ridge where he went bellydown to crawl the last few feet.

It was a good thing his instincts were still intact, because not a half mile before him and resting in a bowl of grass surrounded by a pine forest, he saw the banditos making their night camp. Very carefully, Clint counted thirteen Mexicans, and his spirits lifted to see Miss Judy was being left alone. She stood apart from the men, and the second thing Clint noticed was that they did not allow her to come close to their horses.

Clint spent until sundown studying the mountain meadow and trying to figure out the best way to approach the banditos' camp. Not only that, but he needed to plan an escape route just in case he failed to spirit the young woman away without rousing the camp.

When the sun slipped behind the western horizon, Clint backed off the ridge, brushed the dirt from his clothes, and returned to his horse. As much as he hated to do it, he used his pocket knife to cut his blanket in half, then in quarters. He took the four squares of cloth and tied them around his horse's pasterns, thus silencing the shod hooves that clipped so noisily against the rocks.

The Gunsmith checked his weapons, though he knew with certainty they were in perfect working order. "Well," he said to himself as much as to Duke, "let's get this over with."

He rode a wide circle around the meadow camp, never coming within a half mile of the fire that flickered so brightly. Because he rode through heavy timber in almost total darkness, the going was very slow. He gave Duke his head and allowed the big gelding to pick his way through the tangle of fallen trees and bush.

When he judged he was in a position nearest the horses, Clint dismounted and moved to the edge of the meadow. The Mexican camp was only about two hundred yards away, and he could hear their Spanish conversation. But unfortunately, he could not see Miss Judy. Clint figured her to be somewhere in the darkest shadows beyond the camp-fire light. One thing for sure, he could certainly need to know exactly where she was sleeping in order to have any chance of successfully pulling off this escape.

Clint waited until very late, and when the conversation began to die and several of the men started to crawl into their blankets, he stepped out of the forest and walked boldly across the meadow. When he was within a hundred yards of the camp, he dropped to the grass and began to crawl ahead, keeping low to the ground.

Every few minutes he would raise his head and see how many banditos were still moving. The moon sailed overhead, and the stars winked like a field of quartzite rock under a bright blazing sun.

He waited over a full hour and then he came to his feet and moved quickly forward at a crouch. His gun rode loose on his hip, and he was ready to shoot anyone who sat up to give the alarm.

His heart was pounding when he moved soundlessly in among them. They were dim figures, appearing almost doll-like in repose with their arms thrown out carelessly and loud snores on their breaths. Clint halted near the campfire and slowly revolved in a full circle. He saw her!

She was lying beside a very fat bandito, and her wrist was tied to his with a stout piece of hemp rope. Clint swore silently. He hesitated and then made his decision. He bent beside the campfire ring and selected a large rock. He picked it up and tested its heft. His reasoning told him that the bandit would probably awaken if he tried to cut the rope. And if the man awoke, he would shout a warning and the game would be all over.

I cannot take that chance, Clint thought. Not with Judy's life or even my own. So moving forward, he came to kneel beside Judy. He took out his pocket knife and placed it beside him. Then, taking a deep breath, he clamped his hand over her mouth.

Her involuntary scream was muffled but she struggled, and before he could grasp her wrist, she yanked on the rope, and the Mexican beside her was jerked out of his sleep.

Clint swung the rock too late. The fat bandito shouted a warning an instant before the rock smashed him across the forehead. His warning shout died in his throat, but the damage had already been done.

Clint slashed the rope in two. He grabbed Judy and shouted, "Let's get out of here!"

She must have been awake, because she moved fast. Clint saw figures grabbing for their weapons. He heard startled and confused shouts as weary men were suddenly pulled from a dead sleep and fought to understand what was wrong. Clint leaped the campfire, and as he did so, he kicked burning logs and branches with all his strength. Embers shot into the air and scattered over the Mexicans. They yelped and now, as Clint and Judy raced across the meadow, the sound of gunfire filled the mountains.

There was no time to try and capture a Mexican horse for Judy. No time to think but only to run into the blackness.

"Clint!" she cried. "You came for me!"

"Damn right," he said. "But comin' here is one thing, gettin' out of here with our lives is another!"

The campfire had been knocked down and its light almost extinguished. The leaderless Mexicans were shouting and emptying their guns into the darkness, but Clint was sure he and Judy would not be killed this night. Now all that remained was to try and find Duke and then put as many miles between them and the banditos as possible before dawn.

"I love you!" she panted, trying to keep up with him. "Where are we running to!"

"My horse," he said, "but after that, it's anyone's guess."

They found Duke, and Clint untied the animal and then mounted. He pulled Judy up behind him, and they entered the meadow but stayed right along its edge where he knew the Mexicans could not see them against the black backdrop of pine forest.

"How good are they at tracking?" Clint asked as he hurried Duke along.

"Very good, I'm afraid."

"Then it's nothing but a horserace," he said. "But riding double, there is no way we can win."

"Red-Toothed Mountain is just ahead, and there's a hidden canyon my uncle found. If we could reach it without being caught, maybe we could hide and find that gold."

"Are you crazy!"

"Don't shout," she said, hugging him tightly. "We came this far, it's less than twenty miles from here. So if we can't outrun the banditos, we might as well get rich while hiding from them."

Clint shook his head, but the idea had some merit. Besides, he was fresh out of good ideas for this night. "Are you sure you can find that canyon?"

"I swear I can. I saw the Red-Toothed Mountain yesterday afternoon. It's straight north."

"But you were leading the bandits northeast."

"We were on our way to Zamora's camp," she said almost breathlessly. "They were going to trade me to that Apache."

"Don't ask for the wedding invitations to be given back yet," Clint said. "This little mess we're in may get a whole lot worse before it gets better."

# NINETEEN

"Clint?"

"What?"

"Why did you finally leave Union City and come to rescue me?"

"I don't know," he said, watching the daylight flood across the mountains. They were walking Duke now, giving the big horse a breather and trying to conserve his strength in case they were jumped by Apache or overtaken by the banditos. It had been a long and difficult night.

"You must have some idea why you came to save me."

"Maybe I wanted your gold."

Judy linked her arm through his and hugged him tightly. "I'm sure it was more than that. You don't even believe there is such a thing as the Lost Apache Mine."

"That's true enough."

"Then I still don't understand why you came. Could it be you are every bit as chivalrous as my dear father used to be?"

"What does that mean?"

"Don't play dumb with me, Clint. You know perfectly well what that word means."

He smiled because that was true. "I guess I still have a sort of romantic sense of honor," he conceded. "You know, damsel in distress and all that. I also have to live with my conscience. If I let you come out here and get roasted over an Apache campfire, I'd think less of myself."

"I want to tell you where the mine is again."

He glanced sideways at her. The rising sun gave her face a lovely pink glow, and although she had dark circles under her eyes and was too thin and worn, she was really quite beautiful. "Why do you want to do that?"

"Because. If anything happens to me, I want you to become rich. Richer than you have ever dreamed."

Clint suppressed a smile. How come women always wanted to give him a lot of money?

"I don't care about your mine or your gold," he said. "The only reason I'm going there is to hide in this secret canyon of your uncle's, if there is such a thing. It might just be his imagination running wild again."

"Aren't we about to bet our lives that my late uncle was telling me the truth?"

"Yes, but right now, our lives aren't worth much. The way I see it, Judy, we are about at the end of our string. Apaches are crawling all over the place, and there's a whole band of pissed-off Mexicans on our backtrail. I'll try anything before I'll run my horse to death in a race he can't win."

"I agree. But let's stop for just a minute, and I'll show you the map once more. Please. If I died thinking you had done all this for nothing, I would never forgive myself."

Clint smiled because the statement itself was so illogical. "You mean you still have the map on you?"

"Yes." She stopped and bent over. Clint saw her rip the hem out of her dress and extract the thin, rolled-up map.

"Well I'll be," he said, shaking his head in amazement as she unfolded it, "that was clever."

"Thank you. Now, here is Red-Toothed Mountain, which we can now see dead ahead."

"Don't say 'dead' anything," Clint requested. "Right now, I'm a little spooky about words like that."

Judy continued. "A little farther north are the twin lakes he called The Two Moons. See this line?"

"Yes."

"My uncle said we need to follow it ten miles and we come to that sheer rock cliff that faces south."

"I remember that now. Then we ride around it and climb a hill until we come to a valley with lightning-blasted trees at its entrance."

"See, you *do* remember!"

"Yeah, but that was as far as you told me."

"All right," she said, her voice dropping to a whisper as if they were standing in a crowded hotel lobby full of eavesdroppers. "We ride straight up that valley, and it narrows into what appears to be a dead end. Only right here is the secret entrance to a little canyon."

"Can we get Duke into it?"

"I don't know," she said quietly. "My uncle said it was a very small opening. He got his burro inside, but I don't know about a horse the size of Duke."

Clint clenched his teeth. He would not leave Duke unless their lives depended on doing so. It would almost kill him to desert his faithful friend.

"Assuming we get into that hidden canyon, then what?"

"Then there is a river that runs out of the east end. It comes right out of the side of a cliff and there's a big waterfall. We go in behind that waterfall and find a huge maze of caverns."

"I don't believe this," Clint said.

"You had better believe it. My uncle was something of a geologist. He said that the tunnels were made millions of years ago by the same river before it changed channels. And if we follow it under a mountain, always staying to our right, we will find the Lost Apache Mine. A solid vein of gold ten feet wide than runs along the cave for more than fifty feet."

Clint expelled a deep breath. "That sounds like more gold than they have in the entire United States Mint!"

"I know."

Clint turned and looked along his backtrail. No sign of the Mexicans yet. He had covered his trail as best he could and the wrappings on Duke's hooves would have made it almost impossible for them to track Duke over the rocks. But they would be coming. Just as sure as sundown they would.

"Okay," he said. "Let's mount up and see if we can get around this red mountain and past them Two Moon Lakes before the banditos overtake us."

"You hit Escobar very hard. Do you think you killed him?"

"I sure hope so."

She kissed his cheek and put her arms around his neck. "So do I," she confessed.

Clint felt the young woman's slender body tremble against him. He was surprised to feel a stirring of passion in his loins and was ashamed of himself for imagining how she might look fully unclothed. She would be too thin, but the curves were all in the right places.

Shame on yourself for such lecherous thoughts at a time like this! he chided himself. But all morning long, he could not stop those thoughts and finally, he even gave up trying.

# TWENTY

They passed around Red-Toothed Mountain and climbed higher into the mountains. Clint saw beaver in the rivers, which told him that few white trappers or hunters had ever entered this forbidden country.

Neither one of them were prepared for the sheer beauty of what Judy's uncle had called The Two Moon Lakes. They were beautiful, each about three acres in size and set in a vast meadow of grass and wildflowers.

Clint rode Duke right up to the shore and dismounted. He peeled off his shirt, gun, and holster, and then his boots.

"What are you doing!"

"I'm going for a swim and a wash," he said. "It's been weeks since I've seen this much water this clean."

Without another word, he jumped into the lake. The water was so cold it momentarily took his breath away, but it was incredibly refreshing. When he surfaced, he scrubbed the grit from his face and saw Judy hurrying along the shore. "Where are you going!"

"To bathe where you can't see me!"

"I'll be along in five minutes," he called. "We haven't much of a lead."

"I'll be ready."

And she was—almost. She was just stepping into her dress when Clint arrived. She had scrubbed her underclothes with sand and they were piled in a dripping bundle on a rock. Clint whistled with soft admiration, and she whirled around so that he could not see her small but firm breasts. But her backside sure was an eyeful. "Don't you dare peek!" she cried. "A gentleman would turn his head."

"I'm *not* a gentleman," he said with a chuckle. "You keep getting that confused." He studied her bare backside and was sorry when she finally got herself buttoned up to the neck. "You might as well leave those underclothes right there," he said. "We aren't going to have time to let them dry."

"Then I'll bring them along wet!" It was clear that she was miffed.

Clint shrugged. "Suit yourself. Just don't get our blankets wet. It gets cold up here at night."

"I know that."

She scooped up her wet bundle and tromped over to Duke. Clint reached down and helped her swing up behind his saddle. She looked like a sleek, half-drowned kitten with her hair all slicked down and water still streaming down her face, arms, and legs.

"I think you could have given me five more minutes," she said in a curt voice. "And. . . ."

Clint reached down and squeezed her wet thigh hard. Some inner warning was ringing loud and clear. "Shhh!"

He reined Duke around and studied his backtrail. To her credit, Judy said nothing.

"There!" Clint said, pointing. "See that stand of timber about two miles back?"

She nodded.

"Watch it closely."

Minutes ticked by before they both saw the glint of Mexican silver in the sun. Clint heard Judy's sharp intake of breath. She hugged him tightly, and he felt her begin to tremble. Only then did he realize that she had been working very hard to put on a brave air while inside, she was terrified.

He patted her shapely leg, thinking it was a damn good thing that she was too slim rather than too fat. Duke needed every advantage he could get to stay ahead of the banditos. "Even riding double, I think Duke can keep us ahead of them until we reach that secret canyon."

"It doesn't seem possible."

"It *is* possible," he said, reining the gelding north again and setting him into a gallop.

"They see us!" Judy cried. "And they've started to run."

Clint pulled his Stetson low over his eyes. "Turn your pretty back on them, Judy. Watching them come isn't going to help. Just hold on tight and we'll let Duke run."

The Gunsmith gave the black its head, and the big horse began to stretch out and devour the ground. It was ten miles to the sheer cliff that faced south. Duke could not maintain this pace carrying double for that distance. Clint let the horse run two miles and then he pulled him down to an easy trot. Years ago, an old lawman had taught him that the fastest pace over a long distance was a trot, not a gallop. Clint had tested that theory dozens of times and found it to be true. If a man ran his horse hard, he would have to stop every few miles and let it blow. But if a man had enough space and presence of mind to hold his mount to a steady trot, he could cover amazing distances.

The Gunsmith leaned slightly forward in the saddle to keep his weight over Duke's withers as much as possible. He had been chased before, and he had also ridden down a lot of good horsemen. Clint figured that when it came to getting the best out of an animal, he had few peers. But even more importantly, horse for horse, there was none better than the big black between his stirrups.

"I've never been on an animal like this," Judy said.

"He's pretty special," the Gunsmith agreed.

Duke was blowing hard when they passed under the big rock cliff and began to climb toward the valley marked on Judy's map. "I think this is where we need to unload and do a little running of our own," he said.

Judy understood. They piled off Duke and struggled up the steep grade as best they could. Judy wasn't up to her normal strength and, with the altitude and thin air, she was soon falling and gasping for breath.

Clint looked back. The Mexicans were well mounted, and they were excellent horsemen. They had almost cut the distance in half. Clint knew that if he and Judy did not keep distance between them, the Mexicans would see them enter the secret canyon and all would be lost.

He picked up Judy and threw her up into the saddle, and then he grabbed Duke's reins and ran with all of his might. The incline up the valley was almost two miles long and it was a killer. Clint could hear the breath surging through Duke's distended nostrils.

Run, he told himself. Their horses have to be dying, too!

When he staggered over the hill and gazed down into the valley, the Gunsmith saw the lightning-blasted stumps that he had been told to expect. Seeing them gave Clint a surge of hope, because everything that Judy's Uncle Moses

Malone had drawn on his treasure map was turning out to exist. Clint did not give a damn about the gold, but he sure was counting on that secret canyon to save their bacon. He studied the little valley and saw how it narrowed into a seeming box canyon. "Does the map show *exactly* where that secret entrance is located?"

"No," Judy said, her voice stretched with desperation. "But Uncle Moses said you had to go to the very end and then a little ways up into the rocks. He said it was behind the stump of a big pine tree and hidden with manzanita and brush."

Clint glanced back at the banditos. They were spread out now in almost a skirmish line but still far beyond rifle range.

"I don't think we can find it without them seeing us," Clint decided out loud. "And if they see us and discover the secret entrance, we have lost."

"But what can we do?"

"Keep running!" Clint shouted. He swung up behind Judy and spurred down into the valley. It did not appear to be very long, and there was no reason to save his horse's reserves because this was where their real fate would be decided.

Duke responded magnificently. The big gelding flattened out and ran like the prairie wind. They hit the valley floor and headed toward the secret tunnel with the wind blowing hard across their strained faces.

# TWENTY-ONE

Duke was starting to falter by the time they reached the end of the valley. Clint could feel the big horse's stride getting very short and choppy, and he knew that meant Duke was laboring on reserves and that he could not run much farther carrying two riders.

"Over there!" Judy cried. "I see a big stump!"

"I see a lot of big stumps!" Clint answered as they came to the end of the valley whose walls had grown steep and rock-strewn. The valley had really become a box canyon, and Clint had no doubt that the Mexicans figured that they had their quarry treed.

He reined Duke into cover, and they dismounted before the big horse had even come to a trembling standstill. Clint tied the gelding and yelled, "You search for that opening, and I'll hold them off!"

Judy vanished into the heavy brush, and Clint yanked out his Winchester and then flattened behind a thick pine tree. He levered a shell into the breech of his rifle and then aimed and knocked a bandito right out of the saddle. The others reined their mounts toward cover, and Clint hit two more before they vanished into the rocks and trees. He ducked and ran ten yards as a swarm of bullets came ripping into the pine where he had just been.

"You find it yet?" he called frantically.

"No. Just keep them occupied for a while."

Clint nodded. Two Mexicans were dead and he had winged a third. They were furious, but they sure understood that they were up against an expert rifleman. There were no fools or heroes among the banditos. They were coming at him, but they were doing it very carefully.

Clint could hear Judy crashing around in the brush. She was back in the trees and out of sight, somewhere higher up the sides of the rock walls. He hoped she could find it quickly because the Mexicans were in no mood to strike a deal. Clint had drawn first blood, and these men were intent on revenge. The fat one who was their leader was exhorting them to charge, but the banditos were having none of that. They no doubt figured that time was on their side. To their way of thinking, Clint and Judy were trapped in this box.

"I found it!" Judy cried.

Clint smiled tightly. "Is it big enough to get a horse through?"

There was a long pause and then Judy came down to him. "I'm afraid not, Clint."

"Damn!" he cursed. "I don't want to leave that horse, Judy."

She said nothing.

"Isn't there some way I can enlarge it enough to squeeze Duke through?"

"Not without dynamite or tools," she said, coming back to help him fight.

Clint shoved his rifle at her. "Here," he said, "keep

them occupied for a few minutes. I need to see that opening myself."

"It's right up there behind that tree. About thirty feet up the slope."

The Gunsmith took the slope on the run. He scrambled up loose rock and, sure enough, there was an old stump like Judy's uncle had described. It was hollowed out and filled with termites and wood ants. By the looks of it, the thing would crumble and fall apart within the next few years. Clint, his breath tearing in and out of his chest, his boots slipping on loose rock and rolling gravel, clawed his way upward until he came to a thick stand of manzanita. He knelt on the rock and found Judy's footprint and ducked into what appeared to be nothing but a small animal trail. He crawled ten feet and then crouched before the tunnel.

His heart sank. He could not imagine how Uncle Moses had managed to get a burro through the hole, because it was scarcely wide enough for a man.

"Damn!" Clint said, slamming his fist against the rock in helpless fury.

He heard a sudden volley of gunfire, and then he heard Judy yell, "Clint! They're coming!"

The Gunsmith whirled around and came tearing out through the manzanita. His face was scratched and his arms were bleeding, but he scarcely felt anything as he charged down the canyonside.

"Judy!"

A bullet answered him and then another. Clint dove for cover as splinters of rock and bark exploded over his head. "Judy!"

The guns fell silent. Sweat trickled down the Gunsmith's scratched face, and he waited anxiously, hoping that his worst fears would not be realized.

"So!" a thick voice boomed. "You are the famous Gunsmith, eh! Well *I* am also famous. My name is Señor

José Luis Ortega Escobar, and I am the greatest bandito in all of northern Mexico."

Clint did not move.

"I have the pretty virgin with me. She is alive, but unfortunately, she suffered a little bullet wound. It was an accident, of course. Neither I nor my fine men shoot women—at least not young and pretty ones, señor."

Clint rested his forehead on his arm. He had lost. They had Judy, and he knew that he had to go down to them or they would torture or rape her. Clint knew exactly how things would progress from this point on and that the chances of his own survival were nil.

Escobar's next words bore out his grim expectations. "The señorita is bleeding a little. If you don't throw down your pistol and rifle and come down here *muy pronto*, she will bleed faster."

"Don't come, Clint! Don't. . . ."

Her words ended jarringly. Clint heard the sharp slap of flesh against flesh, and then he heard her moan.

"I'm coming," he said.

# TWENTY-TWO

Escobar was holding a gun in each of his chubby fists, and his men were armed to the teeth when Clint surrendered with his hands over his head.

"Manuel, take his gun!" Escobar ordered. "Search him very carefully."

A tall, thin Mexican with a saber scar down one side of his face jumped forward, and he was shaking with hatred.

"You killed my amigos, gringo!"

Clint shrugged. "They tried to kill me first, señor."

The man's control snapped, and he backhanded the Gunsmith. Clint staggered but did not go down. He heard Judy yell, and then he planted his feet and drove an overhand right into the Mexican's nose. It broke with a sickening crunch, and Manuel howled as he hit the dirt and went sprawling.

Escobar said, "Very brave and very foolish."

Manuel picked himself off the ground and reached for his gun. But Escobar stepped into the line of fire. He spoke not only to Manuel, but to all of his men. "I will decide when and how this famous Gunsmith dies. *Comprende?*"

The Mexicans nodded in reluctant agreement, but their smoldering eyes told Clint that they would kill him at the very first opportunity.

"Juan," Escobar barked, "search and disarm him!"

Clint's gun was yanked from his holster. He carried a hide-out derringer and his knife and they found those, too.

"So," Escobar said, limping forward. "The rattlesnake is defanged."

Clint said nothing.

Without any warning at all, Escobar lashed out and sent the barrel of his gun crashing against the side of Clint's jaw. The Gunsmith felt his legs buckle, and he dropped to his knees.

"Stop it!" Judy cried, breaking free of the man who held her and throwing herself at the Gunsmith's side. "Don't hurt him anymore."

Escobar had been about to drive a boot into Clint's face, but now he changed his mind. Hooking thumbs into his gunbelt, he smiled. "So, the virgin, she loves the viper. Very interesting. What is his life worth to you, señorita?"

"I don't have anything left to give. You've already taken everything."

"Not everything. I have saved the best for the great Apache chief, Zamora. Besides, I think you came into these mountains for a very important reason."

Judy glared at him with defiance. "I told you that we were searching for gold."

Escobar's little black eyes narrowed to slits. "You would not come to such a dangerous place just to search for gold. Even a fool would know better than that. No, I think . . . I think you *know* where there is gold. Eh?"

Judy shook her head. "That's not true." Even to Clint, it was obvious that she was an awful liar.

Escobar shrugged. He turned back to Manuel, who was cupping his broken nose in his hands. With a voice as casual as if he were commenting on the weather or time of day, Escobar said, "Manuel, I now give you permission to slit the Gunsmith's throat."

Clint's belly turned into a ball of ice. He had faced death many times and even expected to die by the gun. But to have his throat cut and to die slowly was a terrible fate —one he vowed not to accept. He knotted his fists, intent on going down fighting.

"Wait!" Judy cried. "If I tell you where there is a lost gold mine, will you let him live?"

Escobar threw his arm out to block Manuel's progress, saying, "Manuel, is revenge so sweet that you would rob us all of a fortune in gold?"

"Sì!"

Manuel was crazed with rage. He batted his leader's forearm aside and lunged at the Gunsmith. Clint had been expecting this. The bandito was beyond reason. The knife thrust was aimed for his belly but Clint twisted and Manuel's blade missed. Before Manuel could recover his balance, Clint grabbed his wrist and smashed it down on his knee. The knife spun away harmlessly, and Clint knocked the Mexican down once more.

"Bravo!" Escobar cried. "I could not have done it better. But I was wrong to think you are completely defanged."

"I won't be slaughtered like a pig," Clint told him. "Not by any man."

But now Manuel was completely out of his mind with pain, humiliation, and rage. He drew his gun and screamed at both Clint *and* his leader. Clint swallowed dryly. He wondered which one of them he intended to shoot first.

One of the banditos solved the issue with a single bullet from his pistol. Manuel died trying to raise his gun and shoot his leader.

José Luis Ortega Escobar blinked and licked his lips nervously. Clint had seen fear in men so great that it could be smelled and right now, he could smell Escobar's rank fear. He watched the bandit pull a silk handkerchief from his back pocket and mop sweat from his round face.

"Arturo," Escobar said, forcing bluster into his voice in an effort to hide the fact that his nerve had been found lacking, "you will be rewarded with Manuel's share of his lost gold mine!"

Arturo grinned and displayed a gold tooth. He blew the smoke from his gunbarrel and said, "You are very generous, my leader. *Muy gracias.*"

"*Por nada,*" Escobar replied. "It was nothing."

He turned to Judy. "Well, señorita, are you ready to show us the gold mine now?"

Clint and Judy's eyes met. "What will it gain you?" he said quietly.

"Your life."

"They will kill me as soon as they find the gold."

She looked away quickly and there were tears in her eyes. Clint saw her square her thin shoulders and then point up the side of the canyon wall. "Up there behind a tree stump is the entrance to a hidden canyon that lies just beyond these rock walls. Somewhere in that canyon, there is gold."

"This is true?" Escobar asked, failing to hide his excitement.

"Yes."

"I will kill this man a thousand times if this is not true," Escobar warned.

"I know that. But it is true."

Escobar spun around on his heel. "Miguel, Raul! Go up and find this secret place. If it is there, come back to me at once."

The two banditos leaped forward to obey his orders. Clint expelled a deep breath and wondered if he had any chance of grabbing Escobar's two pearl-handled guns and somehow getting himself and Judy out of this mess alive.

He decided there was no chance at all. But Judy had bought him a little time. They would need to crawl through that narrow space into the hidden canyon and then search for gold. The Gunsmith knew that Escobar's fuse was very short. If gold were not found almost at once, then the game was over.

Minutes later, Miguel and Raul came rushing back down. "It is there as the señorita says. But it is covered with brush. We will need to clear it away with machetes."

"Then do it!" Escobar said impatiently. "And hurry!"

They waited. Clint listened to the sound of the banditos as they hacked away the manzanita and cleared an opening to the small fissure in the rocks.

"I have always wanted to be rich," Escobar said. "Maybe you have brought me great good fortune, señorita."

Judy said nothing.

"Señorita, I have a proposition for you. I am a handsome man, no?"

She was smart enough to humor his vanity by not telling him that he was a pig.

Escobar drew a cigarillo from his leather vest and began to strut back and forth. "I tell you something, señorita. If you make me rich, I will do you the great honor of taking you as my own woman."

He stopped, lit his cigarillo, and squinted at her through the smoke that trickled from his nostrils. "Believe me, señorita. You would kiss my feet every morning to be with me instead of becoming an Apache slave. Zamora would kill one of such fragile beauty as yours. You would not last a month in his camp."

"What about Clint?" she asked in a ragged voice.

Escobar waved his cigarillo expansively and winked. "I might spare his life if you earned it in my bed."

"Tell him to go to hell," Clint growled.

"You shut up!" Escobar yelled. "Or I will kill you right now!"

Clint clamped his mouth shut.

Judy said, "If you let him go, then I will do your bidding."

"No!" the bandito said. "You must first earn his life."

Raul appeared. "The opening is ready. But it is very small."

"How small?" Escobar asked.

Raul hesitated, but Clint could see the man measuring his leader against the size of the entrance. Escobar would fit, but Clint figured they might have to grease him up like the pig he was before they shoved him through.

Raul started to answer, but suddenly his mouth fell open, and he gasped, "Zamora comes!"

Clint saw at least eighty mounted Apache Indians come streaming up the valley.

Escobar went pale. He shouted up to his men. "Cover the secret entrance! Hurry! They must not find the gold!"

Clint's hands were bound behind his back, and he could hear the banditos working furiously up above to re-cover the secret entrance. Moments later, they came flying down to stand beside Escobar. An hour ago, the banditos had looked very fierce, but now, with the arrival of the Apache, they seemed pitiful indeed.

"Is it hidden?" Escobar asked, raising his hand in a gesture of peace to the approaching Indians.

"Sì!"

Escobar nodded. He pushed Judy behind his wide body to partially block her from the sight of the Apache. "I do not know if I can save you from Zamora," he admitted in a low voice. "I do not even know if we can save ourselves."

Clint shook his head. Things did not look good at all.

# TWENTY-THREE

When Zamora raised his right hand in the sign of peace, an audible sigh of relief could be heard from the banditos. Escobar was almost giggly he was so happy that the Apache leader wanted to talk.

"Amigos," he called to his companions, "dig a firepit and butcher two horses for Zamora and his friends!"

Raul nodded and the banditos quickly went to work to prepare a feast of roasted horsemeat for the Apache leader.

Clint could see why Zamora was so greatly feared. He was a very large man, barrel-chested and long-limbed. He was clad only in breeches and knee-high leather moccasins. His torso was scarred, and there was a terrible, festering wound on his right side, just above the hip. It had the appearance of gunshot, but Zamora dismounted and strode forward as if the wound did not even exist. Clint had heard legendary stories about how the Apache had trained their minds to ignore pain and now he believed them. If he

144

had been suffering an open wound like Zamora's, he'd have figured he had one foot already planted in the grave.

Zamora stopped about ten feet away and to one side of Escobar. The big Apache chief folded his arms across his muscular chest and waited. Escobar had no choice but to go forward to greet Zamora and when he did that, the Apache had a clear view of Judy and the Gunsmith. But mostly, he looked at Miss Judy. Clint saw interest flare up in the chief's black eyes. The Apache were normally inscrutable men, but at the sight of the white woman, Zamora betrayed his desire.

They shook hands, and then Escobar began to speak in the Apache's language. Clint understood little of what was being said and it appeared that he was not alone, for the banditos were working furiously to prepare a feast as quickly as possible. They were in possession of a spade, and they used it to dig the hole and fill it with scavenged wood. Two thin horses, probably Manuel's and one belonging to another of the banditos that Clint had killed, were brought over to the firepit. Without a moment's delay, both horses were shot and quartered by the Mexicans.

In less than fifteen minutes, the raw meat was sizzling on the fire, and its stench was quite unlike anything Clint had ever smelled. Perhaps it was the manzanita with its still green wood and leaves that fouled the mountain or maybe it was just the horsemeat itself. Whatever it was did not sit well with the Gunsmith. He resolved that if he was still alive when it came time to eat, he would pass.

Judy seemed to feel the same way. Left alone while the two leaders argued and talked in the Apache language, she shifted over beside Clint, and every time Zamora glanced over at her, she swallowed with fear.

"I'll kill myself before I'll go with that man," she vowed.

Clint nodded. He was totally absorbed in trying to interpret the conversation between Zamora and Escobar. There were a few Spanish words used and a great deal of sign language, enough so he could follow the general flow of what was being said.

Zamora wanted to know what the banditos were doing up at the end of this box canyon. Escobar kept trying to explain they were just looking for new hiding places, but Zamora did not believe him and was growing increasingly annoyed. Zamora pointed a finger right at Judy and wanted to know who she was. He asked Escobar for her. Escobar shook his head and tried to refuse.

"Their voices are getting angrier," Judy said. "It's not going well, is it?"

"I'm afraid not," the Gunsmith replied. He looked beyond the campfire toward the war party of Apache. It was clear that they were tense and expecting trouble. The warriors held their rifles close to their bodies and kept their hands next to the trigger.

Clint expelled a deep breath. "The problem is this. Escobar fears that if he gives in to Zamora and allows him to have you, he will not be able to find the gold in that secret canyon. That is the *only* reason he is refusing to give you away."

"Look, here he comes."

Escobar did not turn his back on the Apache leader but backed up until he was close to Clint and Judy. "He wants you very much, señorita. I may have to give you to him, or we'll all be slaughtered."

"You do that and you'll never find the lost gold mine. That fissure in the rock is only the first key. There are more."

Escobar swore softly. "Tell me where it is, and I will buy you back from him, señorita! It is our only chance."

"No." Judy shook her head, and Zamora's scowl

darkened but she did not care. "If you find the gold, Clint
and I are both as good as dead."

"And if you don't—"

Clint interrupted. "They lady said no, Señor Escobar.
You must give Zamora something else."

Escobar's face contorted with rage. "He wants this
woman! That is *all* he wants."

"Tell him he can't have her," Clint said. "Tell him that
she is my woman."

"Then he will kill you himself."

"Or I will kill him, and you might find whoever takes
his place is more reasonable. You have everything to gain
and nothing to lose, señor."

"He would cut your heart out and eat it raw," Escobar
said. "Besides, even if you did get lucky and killed him,
the second leader might even be worse."

"Can we afford not to at least try?"

"Have you ever fought with a knife before?"

"No," Clint said. "But I'm a fast learner."

"If you lose, then Zamora will have claim to the señorita, and there is nothing I can do to stop him from taking
her."

"There is nothing you can do to stop him right now,"
Clint said flatly.

Escobar's round shoulders slumped with defeat. "You
are right. If we fight, there are too many of them and too
few of us. Even if you swore to help us, we would still be
overrun and slaughtered. I am too important to die so I will
tell Zamora what you said."

Clint expelled a deep breath. There was nothing to lose.
And he would sure rather go down fighting Zamora than be
tortured to death by the Apache.

At least now he had a chance.

But Zamora didn't think Clint had a chance at all. When
Escobar explained what Clint had said, the Apache chief's

lip curled with disdain, and he barked a guttural challenge
and raised his clenched fist.

"I guess that means he wants us to fight for you, Judy."

She gripped his arm and said, "If he gets you down, I'll
try to kill him myself."

Clint wished he could tell her something profound or at
least comforting, but he couldn't. If he lost to Zamora, he
would die very suddenly. But even if he was victorious,
there was every chance that he would still die.

He held the girl for a moment and whispered, "Win or
lose, you should never quit fighting. Your father didn't,
and he'd expect the same from you, Judy. Think about
that."

She kissed him on the mouth, and Escobar untied his
wrists. The bandito drew out his own knife and said, "I
have killed six men with this blade. Let Zamora be number
seven."

"You know I'll do my best," Clint said.

He took the big knife and liked its feel. The weapon was
patterned after a bowie knife, with its blade length about
fourteen inches and its solid hilt wide enough to protect the
hand when steel clashed with steel.

"Señor, since you have a stake in this," Clint said, as
Zamora drew his own blade and began to draw a large
circle in the dirt, "any helpful advice you'd like to give
me?"

Escobar looked at Zamora. "I think your only chance is
to throw your knife and hope that it kills him before he can
reach you."

Clint shook his head. Whenever one knife fighter was
outclassed by another, the thought of getting in a lucky
throw was considered. But Clint rejected the idea. It took
years of practice to throw a knife well. And even then, if a
man was throwing at a target moving forward or backward,

there was no way to be sure his blade and not the handle would strike first.

"Don't step out of the circle or let him throw you out."

"And if I do?"

Escobar shrugged, "Then you give up the right to defend yourself, and we find out how loud you can scream when he peels off your skin."

Clint tried to swallow but his mouth was so dry, he couldn't even work up a decent spit. At least, he thought bleakly, that business about the circle is a good piece of information to have.

With great reluctance, he stepped over the line into the fighting ring. Zamora stood on his toes and began to weave back and forth. The Apache moved forward to join the Mexicans in ringing the edge of the circle. Judy turned her back on the ring and was unable to watch.

The Gunsmith had fought with guns throughout his life. But he had never expected to have to do so at this point. He was sure that any one of the Mexicans or Apache who surrounded him were far more skilled at this kind of fighting than he was. Still, he knew that he had extraordinarily fast reflexes and that the same physical and mental qualities that had allowed him to survive so many gunfights would somehow come to play in this circle of death.

What he hoped to do was to disarm the big Apache and then bargain for his and Judy's life in exchange for mercy. It might work. Despite all the stories, even an Apache enjoyed life enough to swallow his pride and strike a deal. One thing for sure, no one was going to call a defeated Zamora a coward. The man had too many battlescars to prove things otherwise.

Zamora lunged. Clint threw himself sideways, hardly able to believe how fast the Indian had moved. Zamora came at him again. This time, the big Apache feinted, got Clint to commit and then he drove his blade at Clint's side.

The Gunsmith twisted but felt the steel rip into the muscles across his ribs. He grunted and slashed. His blade cut the Apache across the chest and drew blood, but before he could strike deeper, Zamora threw him to the dirt and jumped at him.

Clint rolled and came up fast. Zamora was enraged more than hurt. His chest wound bled copiously, but it was obviously not deep and wouldn't give Clint the advantage. But now, the Apache who faced him was more cautious. The other Indians around the ring were calling to Zamora, exhorting him to attack and finish the white man.

Zamora feinted again only this time the Gunsmith did not react. Zamora drove his foot up and it caught the Gunsmith alongside of the knee. A jolt of pain speared up through his body, and Clint felt his leg go out from under him. Zamora dove at Clint, and the Gunsmith dropped his own knife and managed to get his hands on Zamora's wrist. The heavier, more powerful Indian chief was on top of him now and pressing his blade toward Clint's throat.

The Gunsmith's arms bulged with straining muscles. Sweat popped out across his face, and he felt as if his eyes were going to burst from his skull. But despite everything Clint could do, as the knife crept downward, he understood that he could not stop the Apache's blade from its inexorable path down through his neck. Clint threw his legs up and hooked his heels under Zamora's chin, then using his powerful leg muscles, he slammed the big Indian over backward.

They both came to their feet, but Zamora was just a fraction of a second faster. The big Apache screamed a death scream and kicked out, but this time Clint jumped straight up and drove his fist into Zamora's face.

The Apache staggered, and Clint reversed his grip on his knife and drove a sweeping uppercut that connected to the stronger man's injured side. Zamora grunted in pain and grabbed his wound, and that was when the Gunsmith smashed him in the ear and sent him flying from the ring.

He had won, or had he merely delayed his own death for a few seconds? Apparently, the latter was the case because Zamora grabbed a rifle from one of his men and slammed it to his shoulder. He pointed it at the Gunsmith and started to pull the trigger.

Clint listened to his final heartbeats and waited, unafraid.

When the rifle barked, he tried not to tense for the impact but he did, and that was when he realized he was still on his feet and still very much alive. But that was sure going to change in one hell of a hurry if he didn't move fast.

Clint saw Judy lower her smoking rifle, and then Zamora pitched over dead. When his body struck the earth, all hell broke loose. The Apache went crazy and the Mexicans opened fire. Clint threw himself out of the circle. It sounded like the Battle of New Orleans as both Indians and banditos fired as rapidly as they could pull their triggers.

Clint grabbed Judy and shoved her toward the mountainside. "Let's get out of here!" he shouted. "The banditos haven't a prayer!"

With bullets slicing all around them, they disappeared into the rocks and trees and ran for their lives. Clint's chest was heaving in and out as they rounded the stump and then threw themselves the last twenty feet up to the layer of manzanita blocking the secret fissure in the rock.

"Go on through!" he urged, grabbing a piece of the brush and racing back to the stump where he began to furiously wipe out their tracks. Clint had no illusions that this would stop the Apache from finding his escape route. But it might delay them an hour or two, just long enough to duck under that waterfall Uncle Moses had told Judy about.

"I have to wait," Judy said as he finished brushing the tracks away. "Listen!"

They both heard it, and it raised the hair on the back of Clint's neck. It was the Apache cry of victory and death. The battle was over. The enemy was vanquished, but there would be friends and blood brothers dead as well.

Clint turned Judy around and pushed her into the rock fissure. "We won't have much of a head start," he told her. "Once the scalping is done, they are going to remember there was a white woman. They'll be on our scent like hounds after fox."

Judy nodded. "All we need is enough time to escape into the mine itself," she told him. "That's all we need!"

Clint heard another Apache cry, and this one was high and quavered in the clear mountain air. He shoved Judy ahead. No one had to tell him that it was the cry of the hunt.

# TWENTY-FOUR

The fissure was deep, and it did not widen for almost sixty feet. Clint looked up at a thin wedge of blue sky and knew that they were walking through an entire mountain. He had never seen such a cleft in rock as this one. It was as if God Himself had used a machete and sliced through this mountain.

"I wish I had grabbed a couple more guns," he said, thinking about the Apache who were probably scouring the mountainside hunting for tracks—and somehow finding them. "Whose rifle is this?"

"Escobar's. He was so absorbed by your knife fight that he didn't even see me take it until I had shot Zamora."

It was a good weapon. An excellent Winchester and fully loaded.

"Clint, do you think we have a chance?"

"It all depends." Clint tried to sound hopeful, even though he knew that the odds were still long against their survival. "They'll be after us now, but at least they can't run us down on horses."

"Oh, look what we have found!"

Clint stepped out of the rock behind her and entered the hidden valley. Despite the fact that his leg was throbbing and his old arm wound had reopened, he smiled. "It's like a lost paradise. It's beautiful."

"And there's the waterfall at the far end."

This late in summer, the waterfall was probably as thin and misty as it got all year. That bothered Clint because it meant that the Apache might be able to see a tunnel right in behind it and realize where their quarry had gone.

The waterfall wasn't high, either, maybe only about sixty feet where it surged right out of the rock. Clint gauged the distance. The valley was like a square hole punched into the Chiricahua Mountains. Its sides were each about a mile in length, and all four walls were composed of about a hundred feet of red crumbling rock with trees hanging off its rims, and here and there, off their sides. The floor of the valley was covered with meadow grass and trees.

"A mountain goat couldn't get in and out of here," he said, taking Judy's arm and hurrying down toward the glistening stream.

"Well, deer sure have," Judy said, as a large doe and her two speckled fawns darted out of the trees to stare wide-eyed at them for a moment and then go bounding off into the forest.

As Clint half-ran, half-hobbled across the valley floor, he saw a lot of deer sign. It genuinely troubled him to think that he was the one that would be introducing the Apache to this magnificent little park, where they would no doubt eliminate the deer in a single hunt.

But that could not be helped, for Clint knew that their own lives were in serious jeopardy, and that they hadn't a minute to lose. If the Apache came through that rock fissure and entered this valley in time to see him and Judy disappear through the waterfall, the game would be over.

"Let's run into the stream to cover our tracks," Clint shouted, hitting the water and sending a spray into the air. He took Judy's hand, and they galloped and struggled up the center of the stream, trying not to splash any more water than necessary, because the warm rocks might not dry completely before the Apache appeared.

They came to the waterfall and its deep pool. Clint looked back and just when he thought that they were going to be all right, he saw the first Apache warrior spring from the rock fissure as if spawned by the earth.

"Get down and let's swim for it!" he shouted over the roar of the falling water.

They swam across the churning pool where huge trout darted with surprise. They dove as they reached the falling water, and even then, its driving force spun them like leaves down to the pool's murky bottom. Clint clutched the rifle between his thighs and fought his way up, pulling Judy with him.

At last they surfaced behind the waterfall and gulped fresh air. Clinging to mossy rocks in the freezing current, Judy swept the water from her eyes, stared for a long minute, and then screamed, "Oh, dear God! There's no cave!"

Clint closed his eyes for a minute and then he reopened them, as if giving them a second chance to see what he wanted them to see. Still no tunnel.

He looked back through the thin veil of water and up the valley floor. His vision was a collage of blurred grass and sky, but he could see the Indians pouring into the valley. There was no hope of escape now. That many Apache would have every inch of this small valley searched within twenty minutes.

His rifle was too wet to fire, and the Apache would

quickly locate them hiding behind the waterfall. Clint shoved the rifle up on the wet rocks and gripped the shivering girl. He was filled with bitterness that her Uncle Moses had betrayed them at this last, this very final moment, when it really seemed that they had a chance for survival.

Judy Monroe clung to him. There was so much noise and splashing water that he could not see her tears but he knew that she was crying and broken up by this unexpected misfortune.

"It's not your fault!" he shouted over the water. "It's not your fault!"

"I hate him!" she screamed. "I hate Uncle Moses!"

So do I, the Gunsmith thought, but only because his twisted fantasy has cost you your young, beautiful life.

# TWENTY-FIVE

Clint held Judy and waited for the Apache to find them. He figured this was a hell of a lousy way to die. He was also trying to figure out why Uncle Moses had lied about the cave they would find behind this waterfall. The man had not lied about any of the rest of it and there seemed no reason why he should change his stripes now.

"I'm going explore every inch of rock back here until I'm sure that there is no way out for us," Clint said, unwilling to just wait for the Apache to discover their hiding place. "Don't move."

Clint began to edge his way along the mossy rocks. He found a stick and used it to probe in the poor light. He knew that the water was at its lowest level right now. This was the time of year when the snowpack had long since melted and been swept down to the oceans and valleys. Streams that raged over their banks in the springtime now. . . .

Clint froze. Maybe, just maybe, the pool was several

157

feet lower than it had been when Uncle Moses had discovered the water cave. "Judy!"

He struggled back to find her, because his shouts were useless under this thundering waterfall. She had not moved, and he gripped her arm and yelled, "The water in this pool is low. I think the cave might be above us!"

"Then let's find it!"

Clint nodded. The light was so poor and the rocks so slippery that he knew they were going to have a hell of a time searching for anything. But when Clint twisted around and saw Apache streaming down the valley toward them, he discovered a fresh burst of energy.

Using the stock of the Winchester rifle to locate pockets for handholds, Clint and Judy hoisted themselves out of the icy water and then clung to the rocks with their fingers and toes.

Higher, Clint told himself. Higher!

A rock broke away from his hand and he grabbed wildly for another hold to avoid falling backward under the waterfall. Face up, that amount of water could still crush or drown him.

The higher he inched upward, the darker it became, but all at once he felt a blast of cold air in his face, and he knew that it had to be from a cave.

"I found it!" he shouted, throwing the Winchester up on a rock ledge where it would be safe. "Come on up!"

Judy was trying. He could almost see her clawing at the mossy rocks in a desperate bid to pull herself up to him. But then, she lost her footing and tumbled over backward with a scream that ended very abruptly when she hit the water.

Clint kicked out from the wall and dropped under the waterfall. The moment it struck him, the impact was stunning. It grabbed him and spun him all the way to the bottom of the pool. He couldn't see anything because of the millions of surging air bubbles. Feeling himself being twisted around and around he groped wildly until he touched Judy's cold flesh. He managed to grab her dress, and then he kicked upward powerfully, driving with one arm and both legs back toward the cliff. He thought his lungs would burst before his head finally cleared the roiling surface just behind the waterfall.

Too weak to move, he threw an elbow up over a rock and pulled Judy's head above water while he tried to catch his breath.

Then he heard the Apache yelling. Clint twisted around in the dark shadows and froze. There were at least a dozen and they were bent over and pointing at him. My God! Do they see me?

The Apache began to argue, and Clint allowed himself to sink down into the water until only his and Judy's nose and mouth were above water. Now he understood what a frog must feel like when hunted by men with spears. Clint held Judy tightly and tried to feel if she was breathing, but he could not be sure nor could he dare move. He could see the excited warriors in snatches between the torrents of falling water. They were gesturing and running back and forth looking for footprints.

Finally, the Apache split up and disappeared out of the opposite corners of his field of vision. The Gunsmith grabbed Judy and hoisted her out of the water, propping her against the slimy rocks.

He managed to climb halfway out of the pool and he pulled her over his shoulder and struggled out of the icy pool of water. In sheer desperation, he grabbed anything he could find to pull himself up, and when he finally reached the cave and again felt the downdraft of cold tunnel air, he shoved Judy up and spilled her onto the same rock ledge that he had thrown his useless rifle.

Clint clawed the rest of the way up and lay there in the

chill air listening to the thunder of the water, and his own hammering heart. When he could move, he reached over and rolled Judy over on her stomach and pounded on her back until she began to cough and spit up water.

"I thought I was dead," she finally whispered. "I wasn't cold or afraid anymore, and you brought me back to this."

"I'm sorry," he said, taking a flint out of his pocket and groping for some driftwood that might have been deposited in the tunnel since high water in the spring. When he found smooth sticks along the sides of the cave, it took him at least another ten minutes to get a fire going. The sticks burned but not brightly, and it gave him only enough light to see a few feet into the dark depths of the mountain.

"What's that?"

Clint crawled forward. It was a lantern and on its base were scratched the initials "M.M." "It belonged to your Uncle Moses," Clint said. "Very thoughtful of him."

Clint lit the lantern's wick, and suddenly the entire cave became brightly illuminated. "Look at them!"

Judy looked up at the ceiling and screamed at the thousands of bats hanging upside down.

Clint grabbed and held her. "Shhh!" he said. "Let's not wake them or bring our Indian friends, okay?"

She nodded. "I'm so cold."

"So am I, but there's plenty of wood in this tunnel, so I'll start a fire."

"No," she said. "Let's go on! They might be coming again."

Clint agreed. It had been almost a miracle that the Apache hadn't seen them after Judy's near-fatal drop under the waterfall. If he hadn't found her far underwater, they would have floated out into the pool and been shot or taken captive—if they hadn't already drowned.

"Clint, do you think they'll come?"

Privately, he thought they would, but only after they had searched every inch of the canyon and its walls for human footprints and came up empty. Only then would they finally consider the possibility of a hidden cave behind the waterfall. Young Apache warriors anxious to prove themselves would dive into the icy pool and surface behind the waterfall. They would explore and probably reach the same conclusions that the Gunsmith had reached and make the same discovery.

"I don't know," he said, not wanting to discourage her any farther. "Let's just go on a ways and see if we can find a passage out of here."

"And find my uncle's gold," she said.

"How can you even think of gold after all we've been through?" he said, greatly annoyed at her pronouncement.

But Judy was adamant. "I believe, having gone through everything we have endured, it was meant that we leave these mountains rich."

The Gunsmith shook his head in amazement. "We're a long, long way from leaving anything. Did your uncle ever tell you whether or not there is a way out of here besides going back out under the waterfall?"

"No."

"Then we are in a real bad fix, Judy. Those Apache aren't know as quitters. They'll stay a week if that's how long it takes to find us."

"How long do you give them?"

Clint shrugged and pulled the girl to her feet. "I'd give them until tomorrow morning to find this cave. So we had better be gone by then."

"We will be, but not without our pockets full of gold," she vowed.

Clint did not argue with her. Instead, he picked up his rifle, took her cold and clammy hand, and started into the cave. He had no doubt that they would discover the vein of pure gold that Uncle Moses called the Lost Apache Mine. But the Gunsmith didn't give a piddling damn about that. All he wanted to do was to get himself and Judy safely out of the Chiricahuas with their scalps intact.

# TWENTY-SIX

Remembering that Uncle Moses had been something of a geologist who had theorized these catacombed subterranean tunnels were millions of years old, Clint found himself fascinated by the rock formations. His lantern cast a sickly yellow glow over the walls and ceilings, and he saw bats everywhere. The floor was spotted with bat guano, but the air itself was surprisingly clean, and Clint guessed that meant that there were many air shafts that led to the surface. Finding a new way out of this maze was Clint's highest priority.

"Uncle said to keep bearing to the right," Judy said when they came to yet another branch in the caverns. "Always to the right."

Clint nodded. The floor was also very powdery and little dust clouds of it rose in puffs with each footfall.

"Listen," Clint said, "do you hear that?"

"A river."

"Yes, and a big one," he said, holding the lantern higher

and trying to discern which direction the sound of rushing water was coming from. But at length he gave up, because the sound seemed to come at them from every direction.

"Did your uncle talk about a river?"

"Yes. He said it ran southeast, and he thought he had found it about seven miles from these caverns. But he could not be sure. If it hadn't been so dangerous to be in this area, he would have attempted to chart its underground course by releasing a special dye used by geologists for just such a purpose."

Clint nodded. The cavern was narrowing a little, but it was still big enough for a stagecoach to race through, and there were little white rocks hanging from the ceiling that reminded him of icicles.

"Stalactites," Judy said, stopping and bending to point to similar though much smaller formations on the floor. "My uncle said they can grow into massive columns and look incredibly beautiful."

"What forms them?"

"Water trickling down through the soil picks up lime, salts, and other minerals, and they crystallize." Judy smiled. "At least, that was my uncle's theory."

Clint shook his head. "How did he ever find this place?"

"An old Apache showed it to him."

"An Apache?" It seemed impossible.

"Yes. The man was trying to return to his village in order to die among his people. He wouldn't have made it if my uncle hadn't come along and nursed him back to health. The old man told him about this secret mine as a reward, probably thinking that he would never survive the waterfall, much less the Apache who rule these mountains."

"The old man was right. You told me that your uncle died of an arrow wound."

"Yes," Judy said with pride. "But he also lived to tell me and my father about this mine. And we have lived to see it and become rich beyond belief, Clint."

The Gunsmith grabbed her arm and pulled her roughly around to face him. He had risked his life to save hers time and time again, but he was not ready to throw it away if it could be helped. Not even for a mountain of gold. "I think we had better have an understanding. The Apache *will* come after us. You can bet on that. And they'll fashion torches so that they can see our tracks. We couldn't hide our tracks in this powder and bat shit no matter how hard we tried. When they find us, it is the end, unless we can somehow get out of here."

Judy reached up and kissed his mouth. "Clint, try to understand me."

"I am trying," he argued, "but you're sounding more and more like you have gold fever, and that will be fatal in this situation."

"I know you're right," she said, standing on tiptoes and hugging his neck, "but you have to remember that, for years, my father's fondest dream was that I would be saved from poverty through this Lost Apache Mine. Don't you see, Clint? If I come all this way and go back with nothing, I've failed both my father and my uncle. It's more than just the money. It is a matter of honor. A debt I would carry to my grave."

Clint expelled a deep breath and shook his head almost in bewilderment. "You southerners sure live by a funny code."

"We're dreamers," Judy admitted. "Men and women who will fight to the death, even for lost causes."

"Well, our cause isn't totally lost," the Gunsmith replied, "but it's on real shaky ground, and I sure don't want to get trapped under this mountain and have no place to run. Better to die above ground, with the sun in your face."

"I don't think we are going to die at all. And—"

The words caught in her throat, and she raised a hand and pointed up ahead. "Look!"

Clint spun around, and when he raised the lantern toward the ceiling its light struck the huge vein of gold layered with quartz. The dazzling vision snatched his breath away.

"I've never seen anything the equal of it," he said, staring openmouthed in wonder.

Judy stopped just before the golden wall. She reached out and caressed its surface and then she scratched the ore with her thumbnail. "It *is* pure gold!" she cried, clapping her hands together like a delighted schoolgirl. She threw her head back and laughed. "Bless you, Uncle Moses, they said you were half crazy and drank too much, but I knew you'd never lie to me!"

Clint held the lamp up and studied the immense vein. There was no telling how deep into the wall it traveled. The vein itself might only be an inch or it might be a hundred feet across. But even if it were only an inch, there was enough gold to fill a railroad coaltender.

Judy found a sharp rock and began to chip away nuggets as big as her fist. She filled the pockets of her dress and then she said, "Please, Clint, take some. It's all I can offer you for risking your life for me and my father."

The way she said it made him finally understand that the gold was sort of a reward, one she very much wanted to give him. It was also a vindication of her uncle, whom she had deeply loved.

"All right," he said, knocking pieces of the stuff to the floor with the butt of the Winchester. "But no good will come of it."

"You don't know that."

He began to fill his pockets until they bulged. Anywhere but in Apache country, he would be worth a small fortune. But given the circumstances, he'd have preferred to be flat broke in Union City.

# TWENTY-SEVEN

"Where are we going?" Judy asked.

"We're going to see if we can find a way out of here," Clint said, "while we still have the chance."

The Gunsmith felt ridiculous with his pockets all loaded down with gold nuggets. He would have traded any one of the damn things for a chunk of beef and a cold biscuit. His stomach was growling, and he was so hungry he felt a little light-headed. He cinched his belt right up to the last hole, and his pants still kept slipping down because of the weight of the gold. Now that Judy had her treasure and Southern pride intact, all he wanted was to get the hell out of the Chiricahuas, but not without his black gelding, Duke.

Duke had carried Clint through more bad scrapes than the Gunsmith cared to remember, and he would be damned if he'd abandon that lovable sonofabitch to the fate of starvation and roasted horsemeat. Clint would not do that to a dog, and he was a lot less fond of dogs than horses.

"We can't go back out there!"

Clint stopped and waited for her to catch up. He noticed that the lantern was running low on kerosene. They would be in a fine fix if the lamp ran dry, and they were plunged into the darkness. At least he still had the flint and could light a stick or two, but then he still couldn't see more than three feet in front of his nose. These caves were darker than the inside of... well, they were the darkest things Clint had ever seen in his life.

Clint took Judy's hand and hurried on. He knew that she was having a tough time keeping up with him, but it was nobody's fault except her own for trying to carry out forty or fifty pounds of gold in her dress pockets.

The Gunsmith stopped at a fork in the tunnel. He crouched and examined their footprints in the dust and crushed bat guano. He moved on with long strides.

"Where are we going?"

"It should be dark outside, and I think our best chance is to try and go back under the waterfall and then sort of float to the edge of the pool. We can crawl out and walk the length of the valley and go back through the hidden rock fissure."

"That's suicide! If I jump into that pool of water with all this gold, I'll sink like a stone."

"Then you have a decision to make," he said. "Your life or your gold. Which do you value the most?"

"My life, of course. But... but does it have to be one or the other?"

"You're the one that said you'd sink and drown. Not me."

"I'm beginning to dislike you, Clint. I'm beginning to think you are very heartless."

Clint laughed a real belly laugh without anger. "You finally got that part right. What I am, Miss Monroe, is a survivor. And if you stick with me and do things my way, you might survive, too."

She was fuming but he didn't care.

They reached the waterfall and big pool right at sunset, and Clint edged down the rocks until he could peer through the sheet of falling water. He could see something, though the falls were so loud he couldn't hear anything.

"Stay here!" he shouted through cupped hands. "I'm going to go down closer to the water and have a look-see!"

She nodded and took the flickering lantern along with the Winchester rifle.

Clint edged down the slippery rocks and was almost to where he could get a decent view, when a large rock under his boot broke free and sent him sliding down toward the waterfall.

The Gunsmith clutched desperately for a handhold, but he could not stop his momentum. He splashed into the pool of water, and the gold in his pockets sent him straight to the bottom. He did the only thing he could do and that was to empty his pockets in a mighty big hurry.

Fortunately, the swirling current did not grab him strongly, and he was able to stay against the cliff and haul himself upward.

"Clint!" Judy screamed. "Clint!"

"I'm all right!" he yelled.

But that was wrong because no sooner had he called up to her than all hell broke loose. The Apache were camped around the pool and when they saw him struggling to get out of the water, they opened fire. And if it had not been for that thin sheet of falling water, he would have been riddled.

Clint scrambled back up to the ledge, grabbed the lantern and the rifle and yelled, "Come on, Judy, the last I saw of them they were diving into the water!"

They ran as fast as they could, though that was not very fast given that Judy was trying to haul a fortune in gold away. Finally, Clint got so exasperated with her that he

took big handfuls of her gold and hurled them to the floor
in anger. She screamed like a wildcat and dropped to the
floor, snatching them up again and stuffing them back into
her dress pockets.

Clint picked her right off the ground and threw her over
his shoulder and began to run.

They finally reached the place where they could hear the
river, and that was where Clint made his decision that it
was their only chance for survival. There just wasn't any
choice. Sure, there had to be thin shafts where the dirty
bats and the fresh air downdrafted into these caverns, but
those shafts might run hundreds of vertical feet.

"Where are we going!" she yelled, still hanging helplessly over his shoulder.

"To water!" he called, putting her down and hearing the
first of the Apache yell as they entered the cave.

The lantern was flickering badly and growing weaker
with each passing moment. Clint cussed the damn thing's
timing and kept pulling Judy along behind him as fast as
she could run. Because of his dying lamplight, he was
afraid that he might step into some hole and drop to the
center of the earth. But given the alternative was a horde of
screaming Apache, it was a risk he was eager to accept.

"There it is!" he cried, skidding to a stop beside the
swift underground river.

"Oh, my God!"

"It ain't God," Clint said, "but it's our only chance for
salvation."

"We'll drown for sure!"

Clint had to agree that she was probably right. The river
was swift and in the dying lamplight, they saw it enter on
one side of the cavern and disappear through a tunnel on
the other side. The only good thing was that the river's
flow was obviously down and that meant there would probably be a shallow airspace between the river and the rocks.

Suddenly, the cavern was filled with gunfire, and bullets were ricocheting all around them as the Apache charged forward down the long tunnel. They had fiery brands raised in one fist and guns in the other.

"Jump in!" Clint shouted.

"Not without you holding me!"

Clint hesitated a final moment and then he tossed the dying lantern and the Winchester into the black, flowing water. Absolute darkness dropped over them as if a giant lid had been slammed down on the world.

Bullets still screamed off the rock walls as the Gunsmith grabbed Judy's hand and pulled her close. "Here we go, honey. I sure hope your Uncle Moses was right about this thing coming out somewhere close."

Judy started to yell something, but the Gunsmith jumped into the swift water, pulling her in with him. The powerful current grabbed them like talons and swept them across the cavern and then hurled them into the small water tunnel.

Clint began to roll over and over though he struggled mightily not to. He felt himself being slammed from side to side in the tunnel, and he tried to keep his body between Judy and the rough rock walls.

We'll never make it, he thought. We'll be beaten to death before we are swept even a mile.

# TWENTY-EIGHT

Clint heard her calling him, but she sounded so very far away that it seemed like a better idea to just drift into an even deeper sleep.

"Clint!" She was slapping his already battered face, and now she was rolling him over on his stomach and jumping up and down on his spine.

The Gunsmith groaned and tried to roll her off but he couldn't breathe. All of a sudden, a bucket of riverwater erupted from his mouth, and he gagged as his lungs were emptied. He choked, feeling terrible.

"Clint," she cried, "don't die on me! Not when we've been saved!"

He wished she would go away until he realized where he was and what he had gone through. The rock walls of the tunnel had torn off every shred of his clothing and left him scraped and battered. When he had no more water in his belly or lungs, he hugged the warm sand and felt Judy climb off his back.

"I wish I had a fire to warm you," she fretted. "But the flint you carried was lost. But I did manage to hold onto two fistfuls of gold!"

With a Herculean effort, he rolled over and stared at her. Because he had protected her body with his own, she looked amazingly good. Her dress was gone. She knelt there beside him and tears were streaming down her cheeks.

"Oh, Clint," she sniffled. "I was sure you'd gone and drowned on me. I was just sure of it!"

"Where are we?" he breathed.

"I don't know," she told him. "We came shooting out of that rock wall over there and then the water washed us up on this sandbar. I have no idea where we are anymore."

He tried to push himself up on his elbows, but he found he did not yet have the strength. He was shivering in the cool mountain air, and so was Judy.

Clint said, "Dig us a shallow trench and then line it with a layer of leaves or grass."

Without a word, she dashed off and within five minutes, she had fashioned their crib. Clint eased his body down onto it, and the leaves crunched comfortingly under his bruised flesh. He looked up at her and waited, not sure what she intended to do next and not wanting to influence her decision.

After several minutes, Judy took a deep breath. "I am a twenty-one-year-old virgin," she whispered. "I don't want to wonder about *it* any longer."

Clint laced his hands behind his head. "I feel about a hundred years older than you. I'm not sure this is what you want, Judy."

But she nodded her head. "It is," she told him in a hushed voice. "I wanted you from the first moment I saw you in Union City. That's part of the reason I came to see you that afternoon. And . . . and the Apache might be just over the next hill. We could be slaughtered at sunrise, and then I'd die without being loved by someone as wonderful as you."

He looked up at her. She was too thin but still quite lovely in the moonlight as she knelt shivering like a small girl, clutching her damned gold nuggets in both small fists.

"Put that gold down and come get warm," he said in a gentle voice.

She obeyed the Gunsmith. She carefully placed her nuggets in a small pile, and because the trench was very narrow, she laid right down on him. He pulled her tight to his chest and felt her body mold to his own. She was cold at first, but as he reached down and stroked her back and buttocks, she warmed quickly. When her lips found his, she seemed to melt against him.

Clint's manhood grew hard and long, and he considered that to be an amazing resurrection considering the ordeal he had just survived. He reached down and slipped his finger into her virgin womanhood, and she sighed with contentment. He moved his finger around in a gentle circle until her hips began to rotate.

Her breath began to quicken and when the Gunsmith felt her get slick inside, he reached down and guided himself into her just a little more and then stopped because he feared hurting her if he rushed.

"No," she moaned, "don't stop there. Please, put it all the way in me!"

He obliged her. Gripping her hips with both hands, he rocked his pelvis upward and his rod entered her more deeply. Judy gasped with pain but instead of pulling back like some girls might, she rammed her hips down and impaled herself on his massive tool.

"Oh," she cried, "don't stop!"

Clint stifled a laugh. Stop, hell, he had not even begun to teach this young southern belle the art of making love.

# TWENTY-NINE

They awoke to a day of bright sunshine and made love once more before they crawled out of their bed of sand and leaves. With his stomach growling, Clint searched through the tall grass beside the river until he found a nest of eggs. He added the thick back legs of two bullfrogs and then smiled to find a patch of wild berries. Judy could not stomach the sight of the raw eggs and froglegs, but she gobbled the berries down until her hunger was satisfied.

"What are we going to do now?" she asked, washing her hands in the same swift river that had delivered them from underneath the mountain.

"We find the Apache camp and steal Duke and another horse back, then ride like hell until we put these damned Chiricahua Mountains far behind."

"You make getting back horses sound so easy."

"It won't be," the Gunsmith said. "We have no clothes, no shoes, and no weapons. It won't be easy at all. But it has to be done. We'd die if we tried to walk out of these mountains in the shape we are in now."

Judy sighed. She looked all about her and smiled wistfully. "This is so beautiful here," she said. "I almost wish we could stay awhile. Make love all summer, swim, and be happy."

Clint scooted over beside her and slipped his arm around her narrow waist. "I don't want to go back and see Apache, either," he said, understanding the real reason behind her fear of leaving this idyllic setting. "But these mountains are crawling with Indians. They'd find us within a week and that would be the end of the summer and the end of our lives."

"You're so very sure of that?"

"Yes. It's like most things we fear in life—you can't run away or even hide from them, so you just have to face them and have a showdown."

She nodded, squared her thin shoulders, and said, "All right. Then I guess we go Apache hunting."

"That's right." Clint tried to make her smile. "At least we have the element of surprise on our side. Those Apache have probably never been hunted by a defenseless, naked white man and woman before."

She *did* smile, though he could tell it was an effort. Judy picked up her gold nuggets and Clint rose to stand by her side. He looked around him, and because he had taken a bearing on the North star last night while lying under Judy, the Gunsmith set his course. They would walk slowly because his body was stiff and badly bruised, and Judy was not strong.

But the Gunsmith figured he could find the Apache camp easy enough, and later that day when he picked out the distant Red-Toothed Mountain, he was sure of it.

"We've got to climb that mountain over there, and it'll

bring us right down to where we first found the rock fissure
into the hidden valley."

"Where all the Mexican banditos were slaughtered?"

"Yes."

"But what if the Apache are gone?"

"They won't be," Clint said with certainty. "Remember,
we led them to a hidden valley filled with venison and then
topped that off by showing them a mountain filled with
gold. Whoever replaced Zamora will not be able to get his
horses into the valley to haul out the gold, so they'll make
camp right where Señor Escobar and his men died."

"That seems as if it happened a hundred years ago,"
Judy said. "Not yesterday. My uncle's Lost Apache Mine
doesn't belong to me anymore. It belongs to the Apache."

"It always did," Clint said. "Maybe the new chief of the
Apache will use the gold to help his people, or maybe he'll
just take enough to trade for more guns to raise more hell. I
don't plan to stay in Arizona long enough to find out."

Judy studied the nuggets in her hands. "At least I have
something to show for all this. Gold and having been your
woman last night."

Clint didn't know what to say right then, so he took her
hand and led her toward the mountain they needed to cross.
The rocks hurt the soles of their feet, and the climb was
difficult but not impossible. Halfway up the mountain the
Gunsmith saw a grizzly bear moving through the trees.

"Don't move!" he hissed.

Judy froze at his side. They waited with hearts thump-
ing until the bear vanished from sight before they moved
on. With the clear blue sky overhead and the river a ribbon
of silver down below, Clint smelled the pine and heard the
raucous arguing of bluejays. This was a mighty pretty
country, but he would be more than happy to leave it to the
Apache.

* * *

It was late afternoon when they topped the mountain and limped down through the forest until they could see the Apache camp. Clint's spirits sagged when he counted fifteen Apache left to guard the horses and watch for enemies. He had been hoping that only one or two Apache would remain outside the hidden valley, but now that he saw the great Apache remuda, he understood that those hopes had not been realistic.

"What now?" Judy's voice was filled with anxiety.

"We wait until darkness and . . . there he is! Duke!"

Clint pointed and a wide smile creased his lips. He could pick that big black gelding out of a thousand head of horses. The Gunsmith squatted bare buttock to bare rock and could not stop grinning. Duke stood a little apart from the other horses. He was bigger and stronger than the others, except for one horse who also stood much taller than the Indian ponies.

"I'll bet that's your Thoroughbred, Judy!"

She followed his pointing finger with her eyes and then she also smiled. "That *is* him!"

Clint leaned back on a bed of pine needles and Judy lay down beside him. "We have some time to kill," he said.

Her lips met his and she gripped him tightly. "Then let's not waste a minute of it," she breathed.

Clint agreed. He was going to make love to Judy in plain sight of his enemies. And then he was going to steal their horses.

# THIRTY

Clint grew nervous when the sun went down. He knew that Indians were experts at horsethieving while he was a neophyte, a raw beginner. If he had a gun or a rifle, and maybe some britches to wear and a pair of boots, he would feel a whole lot more confident.

"The way I see this," he told Judy, "is that we sneak down there and try to catch our own horses. If we can do that, we ought to be able to outrun them."

"But how will we rein the animals? They're not Indian ponies taught to turn by knee pressure."

Clint reluctantly agreed she had a real good point. He thought that Duke would respond to knee pressure and get him safely out of that valley, but that wouldn't help Judy on her big Thoroughbred.

"Well, then," he said, "I guess we had better change the plan. What I'll try to do is club one of the Apache guards and then get ourselves a rifle and a couple of horsehair bridles."

"I wish we could get saddles."

"I'll try to get us saddles, too," he decided.

"How are we going to do that?"

"I don't have the slightest idea." Clint patted her on the shoulder. "Judy, win, lose, or draw, it has been a real experience. And if they start shooting at us, my advice is to grab any old horse you can and ride like the wind. It's dark, and you'd have a night to escape or to hide."

"I wouldn't leave you," she said, hugging him tightly.

Clint pushed her away. "Listen, if I was dead or badly hurt, I'd want you to leave. It could happen down there, and there is no sense both of us biting the bullet."

She raised her chin. "All right, as long as you agree you'll do the same if I get shot."

He agreed because it was pointless to discuss the subject any longer. "Come on, let's get down there close so we can move in around midnight when they are asleep."

"Will the guards stay awake all night?"

*"That,"* Clint said, "is the real big question. And since I have never been around an Apache camp at night, I have no idea."

But as they moved down the mountainside, hobbling and limping over the sharp rocks that punished their poor feet, Clint figured he would have the answers to Judy's questions in about three hours' time.

He looked up at the stars. It was well past midnight and the Apache camp was silent. The Indians' remuda was grazing less than eighty feet away and *there were no guards in sight!*

"We may have finally gotten lucky," he whispered.

Judy was crouched beside him. "How are we going to get the saddles and bridles?"

He pulled her close and whispered in her ear, "They must be around here someplace. What I want you to do is to find your horse and unhobble him. Use the hobbles to hold him by the neck and be ready to swing up and run for your life if things go bad."

When she started to protest, he gave her a firm shove away from him. This was not the time or place to debate things. She *had* to do what he asked whether she liked it or not.

The horses were watching them with real interest. Clint could see their heads were up and their ears were cocked forward. Duke had moved close and he nickered softly to his master. But as for the other Indian ponies, so far, none of them had snorted or raised a ruckus. That was a relief, because Clint had heard Indian ponies would nearly stampede at the scent of white people. But then, he and Judy had been through so much hell and high water that maybe their scent had all been washed or scraped away.

Clint decided that each Apache might keep his own saddle and gear beside him at night. That being the case, the Gunsmith took a deep breath and headed into their camp, walking on the balls of his feet.

There was a moon out and it was bright, but it kept ducking in and out of a field of clouds. That made things tricky. One minute you felt like you were walking in among the Apache in broad daylight, the next you were afraid that you might step on one and end this deadly game.

The moon slipped behind clouds just as Clint entered the camp circle of sleeping Apache. Clint took a few more tentative steps and then decided that he had to see where he was stepping before he went any farther. Every second that passed seemed like an hour, but he was fiercely determined to get a gun and at least two bridles before rejoining Judy and the horses.

When the moon sailed out from behind the cloud cover he almost jumped because his big toe was about two inches from an Apache's face. He lifted his foot and backstepped, feeling the sweat course out of every pore on his body.

An Apache grunted and almost rolled across Clint's feet. The Gunsmith swallowed silently and looked up at the moon, which was racing into another cloud.

Hurry, he thought, grab a couple of bridles and a rifle and get the hell out of here before one of them wakes up!

He saw a bridle and reached for it, then moved to another and took it as well. An Apache saddle lay beside its owner and Clint was sorely tempted to grab it, too, but he spotted a rifle and decided to take it instead.

The moonlight was vanishing as his hand snaked out for the rifle. His fist closed over it and he lifted, but suddenly, its owner awoke with a snarl and a scream.

Clint yanked on the rifle only to discover it was tied to the Apache's wrist. With the man's screams in his ears, Clint yanked even harder and the leather thong broke.

The Gunsmith whirled and ran through the absolute darkness. Behind him, the Apache camp erupted in shouts and curses.

"Clint, over here!"

He veered toward Judy's voice and collided hard with a skittish Indian pony that knocked him flying. He bounced up and plunged on.

The moon sailed back out from behind the cloud and suddenly, there they were, exposed and not fifty feet from the Indians. Clint grabbed Judy and threw her on the Thoroughbred. He wrapped a horsehair bridle and rope around the dancing Thoroughbred's arched neck so that Judy might have some control and then he headed the big horse around and sent it racing away into the night. He could hear Judy calling his name over and over.

Something nudged him in the back, and he turned and there was Duke. Clint did not need any further encouragement. He bent and untied the gelding's hobbles, then grabbed a hunk of mane and swung up on the big horse. Bullets seared across the cold night air. Duke vaulted forward so powerfully that the Gunsmith was almost left sitting in midair. The acceleration slid him back to Duke's flanks but he kept his hand in the gelding's mane and pulled himself up close to the withers.

Far ahead of him he could see Judy racing across the valley, her skin very white on her dark horse.

Clint looked back to see the Apache camp boiling like a riled colony of red ants. The Apache would come after them, but Clint believed the chase would be brief because their newly discovered mountain of gold would be an irresistible lure. Just as it had been for Judy Monroe.

Clint wished he had a gun, clothes, boots, and a saddle, but he was so damned happy to be alive he raised his fist to the vanishing Apache and shouted, "Whoo-weee! You'll *never* catch us now!"

They were going to escape with their lives, and he'd bet Judy still had those gold nuggets clutched in her hot little hands. They'd be her stake on a new life, and it was a stake she had richly earned.

As for the Gunsmith, he amused himself by thinking that whoever saw him and that southern gal ride naked out of these damned Chiricahuas was sure going to get an eyeful.

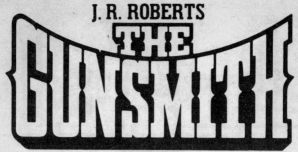

# J. R. ROBERTS
# THE GUNSMITH
## SERIES

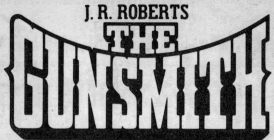

## J. R. ROBERTS
# THE GUNSMITH
## SERIES